MYA's STRATEGY TO SAVE THE WORLD

Tanya Lloyd Kyi

PUFFIN

an imprint of Penguin Random House Canada Young Readers,
a Penguin Random House Company

Published in hardcover by Puffin Canada, 2019
Published in this edition, 2020

1 2 3 4 5 6 7 8 9 10

*Publisher's note: This book is a work of fiction. Names, characters, places and incidents either
are the product of the author's imagination or are used fictitiously, and any resemblance to
actual persons living or dead, events, or locales is entirely coincidental.*

Manufactured in Canada

Library and Archives Canada Cataloguing in Publication

Title: Mya's strategy to save the world / Tanya Lloyd Kyi.
Names: Kyi, Tanya Lloyd, 1973- author.
Description: Previously published in 2019.
Identifiers: Canadiana 2019014534X | ISBN 9780735265264 (softcover)
Classification: LCC PS8571.Y52 M93 2020 | DDC jC813/.6—dc23

Library of Congress Control Number: 2018936946

www.penguinrandomhouse.ca

 Penguin
Random House
PUFFIN CANADA

MYA'S STRATEGY TO SAVE THE WORLD

ALSO BY TANYA LLOYD KYI

Me and Banksy

For Julia,
master of the multi-pronged strategy

ONE WEEK WITHOUT MOM

T HERE ARE TWO TYPES OF PEOPLE IN THE WORLD: those who sleep with tissue boxes on their bedside tables, and those who pick their noses before bed and wipe their boogers on the sheets. I was the first type. My sister, Nanda, was the second.

I knew this because (a) we shared a bedroom, and (b) my mother once read that kids who get more sleep are more intelligent. Which meant I had to go to bed at 8:30 p.m., the same as Nanda (who is FOUR YEARS younger than I am). It was practically still light outside, which meant I could see her wipe her snot on her sheets.

And Mom and Dad wondered why I refused to share a bed with Nanda on vacation. Who would want to share sheets with a known snot-wiper?

On the Saturday night after our second week of school, I was awake for plenty of time to watch Nanda handle her snot, and for a long time after. Mom was away and Dad had a work party to attend, so I was left babysitting. I had been begging them, *forever*, to stop hiring Joanna from down the street because I was twelve years and three months old, almost a teenager myself, and it was ultra-humiliating to be babysat when I wasn't a baby and did not need to be sat upon. I was totally up for the job.

It wasn't easy to supervise my eight-year-old sister, though. At first, I thought Nanda would watch TV and I would call my best friend, Cleo, so we could talk about how Drew cried in the cloakroom at lunchtime after his soccer team lost. But we had hardly started discussing whether Drew was wonderfully sensitive (Cleo's opinion) or weirdly competitive and a bad sport (my opinion) when, from the corner of my eye, I saw zombies. Nanda was watching a show about dead things with flesh still hanging from them. They were staggering around a city as if that was the best thing dead people could find to do with their time.

Nanda always ruins everything.

After I made her turn off the TV and put on her pajamas, she threw a fit.

"Mya, I'm not making this up," she said. "There's something outside the window."

There was nothing there, of course, but I had to open our bedroom window and yell, "Come and get us, flesh-eating figments of Nanda's imagination," before she would believe me. Then I had to stay in our room while she curled up, picked her nose and went to sleep.

I got out my flashlight and read a book until 9:30 as a matter of principle. After that, I lay in the bed across from Nanda's with my eyes wide open, thinking every sound was the creaking of rotten bones. There were a *lot* of sounds outside. I kept popping up to look. Once it was someone skateboarding. Once it was our neighbor parking his car. But there were also noises I couldn't identify. Squeaks and rustlings. It even seemed as if something bumped against our roof.

Eventually, I went downstairs and got the rolling pin from the kitchen drawer and stashed it beneath my bed, so I could defend our home if necessary.

About six billion hours later, Dad's keys jingled in the lock. I closed my eyes and listened to him tiptoe up the stairs, which wasn't quiet at all because his knees went *crackle-crackle-crackle* with every step. (This was also how I knew for certain that he wasn't a zombie.)

Dad paused in the hall and peeked into our room. I pretended to be asleep, of course, because that was the sort of mature, under-control babysitter I was determined to be.

To: p.lwyn@hotmail.com
From: myamyapapaya1@gmail.com
Subject: Breakfast perfection

Dear Mom,
I babysat for Nanda last night while Dad was at his work event. Everything went super smoothly. I am now your trusty, reliable live-in babysitter, available night and day. And while this first session was free, I think you should consider the low, low rate of five dollars per hour. Who can compete with that?

Also, why have you never bought us Toaster Strudels? They are the most delicious things EVER, and Dad says we can have them every single morning until you get home from Myanmar. I know you'll have to stay until Grandma is feeling better, but how long will that be, do you think? Dad might need to buy a few more boxes, and the picture on the back of the box says there are also chocolate and blueberry varieties.

Please kiss Grandma and tell her it sucks that she caught pneumonia (except I know we can't say *sucks* to Grandma, so please reword for me). I hope she heals quickly and you can come home soon. But not too soon because, you know, chocolate and blueberry varieties still to try.

Miss you tons and tons and TONS!

Love,
Mya
xoxoxoxoxoxoxoxoxoxoxoxoxo

ONE DAY, I'LL HAVE AN AMAZING JOB WITH THE UNITED Nations. They'll send me all over the world. I'll fly into countries that have wars and famines. I'll find brilliant solutions. Once everyone agrees to my suggestions, I'll be famous.

I already have plenty of experience with that sort of thing.

Cleo and I sit beside each other in Ms. Martinson's English class, in the prime spot under the windows. Which would be perfect EXCEPT that all desks in her classroom are in groups of four. The other two desks in our square are occupied by Drew and his best friend Ian, and even though we are in seventh grade, not second, the two of them spend ridiculous amounts of time making fart sounds with their armpits and knees.

On Monday, while we were supposed to be working on letter writing, Ian passed a note to Cleo that said, "Cleo wants to kiss Drew." Then Ian started laughing hysterically. Cleo was already turning purple when Drew grabbed the note and added to it. Now it said, "Cleo wants to kiss Drew's butt." I reached for it, but before I could grab the paper, Ian got it back. (This is the sort of thing that UN negotiators have to deal with all the time.) Now, the note said, "Cleo wants to kiss Drew's butt—BAD!" Which wasn't even grammatically correct.

Drew added more exclamation points, and that was when Cleo threw her water bottle at Drew's head.

He clutched at his forehead and wailed like a baby. "What did I do? I didn't even write it!"

Of course I was on Cleo's side, but who throws a METAL water bottle? Plus, who would drink from a water bottle once it had touched Drew's head? Now she'd never be able to use it again, which was a total waste and environmentally damaging too.

By that time, Ms. Martinson was standing over us, pointing to the door. She sent Cleo to see Principal Richards and Drew to the first aid room. Ian folded his hands, smirking as if he were king of the world. So I kicked him in the shin—hard—as soon as Ms. Martinson had turned away.

He yelped, but not like Drew and not loudly enough to get Ms. Martinson's attention.

At least he showed some signs of intelligence.

Drew and Cleo never came back to class, so I put my conflict-resolution skills to use at recess. First, I told Ms. Martinson that her unit on symbolism had been fascinating.

"Your examples of rivers representing the passage of time were very thought-provoking," I said.

My mom is a freelance editor. She says that whenever you have to say something difficult, you should make a "poop sandwich" and put the bad thing between two good things. So after I told Ms. Martinson what an awesome teacher she was, and how I fully supported her decision to send Cleo to the office, I mentioned that there were extending circumstances for Cleo having thrown her water bottle.

"Extenuating?"

"Sure. My point is, there was note-writing going on. It was inappropriate, and Cleo was justified in her actions."

Which is exactly how I'd address the United Nations.

"Thank you, Mya," Ms. Martinson said. "I'll take that into consideration."

"I'm sure that with you in charge, justice will prevail," I said, adding the final piece of tasty bread in my poop sandwich.

I spent the rest of recess organizing the classroom library, so Ms. Martinson could see what a reliable and trustworthy witness I was.

Cleo totally owed me.

I THOUGHT ABOUT WHAT WOULD HAPPEN IF I THREW A metal water bottle at someone's head and got suspended from school for a day. Here's a brief outline:

a) My dad and I would meet with Principal Richards, and Dad would force me to apologize for my behavior.

b) We would drive to my victim's house, where I would have to apologize in person, even if the water-bottle throwing had been *completely* justified.

c) Once in our own living room, we'd have a long family discussion about patience, because Mom grew up Buddhist, and Buddhism is all about patient acceptance.

d) Next, we would have a long discussion about forgiveness, because Dad and his family are Christians, and they're all about turning the other cheek and not throwing stones, or water bottles either.

e) There would be many words about how I'd disappointed my family, and many long, sorrowful looks as Mom and Dad wondered aloud where they'd gone wrong in their parenting decisions.

f) Nanda would walk past the living room as many times as possible, smirking at me every time.

g) I would be grounded for life.

That was what would happen to *me*. Apparently, things were different in Cleo's world, even though Cleo's mom is a police officer, so you'd think she would have high standards in the truth, justice and punishment departments.

Cleo and her mom and Principal Richards had a long meeting, during which Cleo told them a sob story about struggling to adjust to being a tween with her mom working so many long hours and night shifts. The next day, the very day of her suspension, Cleo did not have to go to Drew's house and apologize in person. Instead:

CLEO GOT HER OWN PHONE!

Which basically made me the last person on the entire Earth without proper communications technology. I may as well have been grounded myself. For life.

To: p.lwyn@hotmail.com
From: myamyapapaya1@gmail.com
Subject: The twenty-first century

Mom!! CLEO GOT HER OWN PHONE!!
    Could I have one? It would be very helpful while you're away. After all, what if I'm in an emergency situation? I asked Dad once last year, and he said I couldn't have one until I was thirty-five, but I think he was kidding.
    Please, please, please?
    Hugs to Grandma.

Love,
Mya

To: cleocleobear@gmail.com
From: myamyapapaya1@gmail.com
Subject: AHHHHHHHHHHH!

I STILL CAN'T BELIEVE YOU GOT A PHONE!

ON THE WAY TO SCHOOL ON WEDNESDAY, CLEO SHOWED
me all the features of her new phone. ALL OF THEM.
Because everything she said was, "My phone . . . my
phone . . . my phone . . ."

She could text, take pictures, check the weather, bake
pretend cupcakes and raise a family of dragons. The
dragon game was actually amaZING, but just as she was
explaining how the app notified her whenever a dragon egg
was ready to hatch, Nanda caught up to us on the sidewalk,
stuck her fuzzy head between our shoulders and ruined
everything.

"This should count as part of your screen time," she said.
"I'm telling Dad."

Nanda and I had a strict thirty-minute screen-time limit,
which was torture, and proof that Mom and Dad did not live
in the twenty-first century. It was probably grounds for intervention by social services. How were we supposed to become
educated citizens of a high-tech world when we weren't
allowed to look at screens for more than half an hour a day?

"Shut up, Nanda," I said.

"I'm telling Dad you told me to shut up."

Nanda and I didn't go to the same school, but her elementary school was right beside my middle school, so it was my job to drop her off every morning. Now that Mom was away, I had to pick her up every afternoon too. My semi-Buddhist genes told me I probably did something terrible in a previous life in order to deserve this.

"Look, Nanda," Cleo said, holding out her phone, "I have a *huge* music library." Cleo has curly brown hair and big green eyes. When she opens them really wide, it's as if she's casting a spell. You can't help but agree with everything she says.

Nanda loves music, so she shouldered in right next to Cleo. Which was (a) hypocritical, since she was the one who complained about screen time, and (b) annoying, because Cleo was *my* best friend.

I was left trailing behind them on the sidewalk.

And speaking of being left behind in a friend-less, phoneless state, Mom called last night. She'd seen my email and said she'd talk to Dad about "the phone issue" when she got home. But who knew how long that would be? I asked how Grandma was doing, and Mom said people healed more slowly when they were older.

That wasn't encouraging. Grandma was ancient.

Not having a phone when everyone else did would be like floating around in outer space by myself while all my friends had a dance party in the space station. What if I was stuck in this state for months? Or years? Or forever?

Mom and Dad were living in some sort of time warp and thought I was still ten years old. It wasn't just the phone-less-ness and the screen-time limits. It was my entire existence. For example, we live in a three-bedroom townhouse. Two of the bedrooms are on the top floor, and one of the bedrooms is in the basement. Most parents would allow their almost-teenaged daughter to sleep downstairs, where she could have her own SPACE and INDEPENDENCE and FREEDOM FROM SNOT. But no. Mom and Dad said it was too far away from the family.

It was possible my parents were trying to permanently sabotage my life.

WRITING PROMPT:
THE MOMENT EVERYTHING CHANGED

Mya Parsons, Division 3

My mom is in Myanmar looking after my grandma. You might be wondering how this happened, especially since you just saw my mom at our school's September Open House. Well, there was a moment that everything changed.

It was the day before Mom left, at six in the morning. The phone rang.

This almost always means a call from Myanmar because either (a) everyone in that country calculates the time change wrong or (b) everyone in that country thinks 6 a.m. counts as morning.

I didn't worry about the call at first. But as I was trying to drift back to sleep, the sounds from my parents' bedroom weren't the usual chatting-with-relatives variety. Mom was opening and closing doors. Dad murmured a few things, then left the room and *crackle-crackle-crackled* down the stairs.

Something weird was happening.

My sister, Nanda, and I hauled ourselves out of bed at the same time. We pulled on our robes, then I pulled mine off again because my Auntie Winnie bought us matching fluffy purple robes for Christmas last year, and while I particularly love mine, especially at 6 a.m., I refuse to match my sister.

Nanda made it to the hallway first. "What's going on?"

"Oh, honey, it's early. Go back to bed," Mom said.

"Can't sleep," Nanda said.

"Because you guys are stomping around like elephants," I grumbled, shivering. "Who called?"

"Auntie Pyu from Myanmar," Mom said. I have a vague memory of Auntie Pyu, who is actually some sort of great-aunt. I have a LOT of relatives in Myanmar, and they all kiss me and pinch my cheeks and hand me presents. They tend to blur into one another.

"Grandma's a bit sick."

My grandma and grandpa immigrated to Canada when Mom and her older sister, Auntie Winnie, were kids. But five years ago, after my grandpa died, Grandma moved back to Myanmar. She missed the heat, she said.

"Sick how?" I asked Mom.

"Pneumonia. She's in the hospital. Dad's trying to book a flight right now."

"We're going to Myanmar?" Nanda lit up. She loves Myanmar. And I have to admit I do too: great food, endless sunshine, no school. What's not to love? But it was pretty obvious . . .

"*Mom's* going to Myanmar."

"Without us?" Nanda made it sound like Mom was setting off for Mars and might not return until we were senior citizens.

Mom gave her a big hug. "Oh, honey, I'll call or email you every single day until I'm home. And it won't be long. We'll get Grandma healed as quickly as we can."

It's disconcerting when grown-ups get watery eyes.

"Don't worry about us. We can handle things," I said. Then I glared at Nanda until she wiped her nose on the back of her sleeve (gross) and nodded.

"Who's going to make breakfast every morning?" she said.

Which was okay because it made Mom laugh.

As it turned out, we had breakfast at the airport the next day, then we waved goodbye to Mom as she passed through the security gates and disappeared.

The time between (a) getting the call and (b) dropping her at the airport was just over twenty-four hours.

(By the way, if you're looking for Myanmar on our classroom globe, look for Burma instead. That's the old name for the country. Some people still use it to show they don't agree with the military guys who switched the name in the 1980s. It's also possible our classroom globe is an antique from before the name change happened.)

Nanda,

You left your disgusting, one-eyed Pennybear on my bed again. If you do not keep your stuff on your side of the room, I will bury it in the backyard.

To: cleocleobear@gmail.com
From: myamyapapaya1@gmail.com
Subject: Dryness

What did you get on your English assignment? I got an A, and Ms. Martinson said my piece was "touching," but she also said she liked my use of "dry humor." My essay was totally serious! I think she might be confused.

Also, I got your email about Drew and your theory about his class-clown act being a disguise for above-average intelligence. If that's true, he's an excellent actor. Definitely Oscar-winning.

Was it his shoes or Ian's that smelled so bad yesterday?
I almost suffocated.

I MISSED DAD WHENEVER HE WENT AWAY, AND I MISSED
Mom whenever she went away. Equally. But it was a lot easier when Dad was away and Mom was at home because Mom
knew more. Even though she worked full-time, just like Dad,
she still remembered which days were hot-lunch days at
school, which one of us ate bananas for snack (NOT me)
and where everything belonged.

After dinner on Thursday, Nanda tore apart our bedroom looking for her soccer shin pads. The place looked
so messy, I thought the government was going to have to
declare our house a national disaster area.

"Mya, I need beep-sistance!" she said. My sister refuses
to say the word *ass*, even if it's part of another word. This has
been going on for so long, our whole family now says "beep-
sistance" and "beep-sparagus" without even thinking.

"Look in the laundry bin." It was a good bet, because no
one had done laundry in the week since Mom left.

"I already looked. They're not there."

"Ask Dad."

"He says I have to be responsible for my own things."

This sounded reasonable.

"Mya!" She looked so pathetic that I started to feel sorry
for her. But it was her own fault that she tried too hard in
soccer and made the under-nine elite team, which meant she

17

had to do year-round practice with no winter break like other teams got. (Nanda's soccer league had obviously never read the United Nations Convention on the Rights of the Child.)

"I'm going to be late for practice!"

I double-checked the laundry bin, her dresser drawer and under her bed. No shin pads.

"Nanda, you'll have to go without them." Not that her coach would let her play with no shin pads.

I was talking to an empty room. My sister had disappeared.

"Where are you?"

"In the bathroom!"

I found her sitting on the tile floor, one soccer sock up and one down. Beside her was a box of Mom's maxi pads.

"WHAT ARE YOU DOING?"

"I found pads!" she said. "These'll work. They're even sticky."

She'd peeled the backing from four of them and lined them up in a double layer along her shin. As I watched, she rolled her sock right overtop.

"You can't . . ."

Dad honked, long and loud, from the driveway. Before I could say anything else, Nanda hopped up, brushed past me and thundered down the stairs, leaving me staring at the square blue maxi-pad packages scattered across the bathroom floor.

There was no way I was touching them.

I stomped back to my bedroom, threw myself onto the bed and allowed myself to really miss Mom. She would have known where Nanda's shin pads were and she never, ever would have let my sister leave the house wearing feminine hygiene products.

I was going to have to repress this memory, immediately.

I SHOULD HAVE GONE TO MYANMAR WITH MOM. I COULD have been a huge help with Grandma, and Mom and I could have gone shopping too. Mom was born in Myanmar. We'd all been there a few times, but not since I was nine. On that trip, we went to a massive market that had stalls piled with gold bells and carved wooden elephants and shell necklaces. I also remembered six billion relatives kissing me, everything smelling like sandalwood and a LOT of food. Most days, I thought I was going to pop from eating too much.

Right now, there was violence on the border between Myanmar and Bangladesh because the army was burning the villages of a Muslim ethnic group called the Rohingya. Dad said not to panic, the fighting was far away from Yangon, where Grandma lives. But of course I worried. I worried about Mom because she was traveling without us, and Grandma because she had pneumonia, and the entire Rohingya population because families were fleeing through the jungle toward Bangladeshi refugee camps, which were not exactly five-star resorts. As a future United Nations representative, it was my job to worry.

On my list of other world problems—I might starve.

Mom called on Friday to tell us she wouldn't be staying at Grandma's house anymore. She was moving to a guesthouse closer to the hospital. Here's what I thought: she probably moved because there was a cook at the guesthouse who made all her meals for her. She told me that for dinner she'd had chicken curry, stir-fried watercress and sour soup. I LOVE sour soup, but Mom can hardly ever find the right ingredients to make it.

We seriously could have used a cook around our house. We'd had rice, scrambled eggs and broccoli for the third night in a row, and the broccoli was burnt. Dad said it was caramelized, but I'd never tasted caramel like his before.

I was going to repress that memory too.

To: p.lwyn@hotmail.com
From: myamyapapaya1@gmail.com
Subject: Missing you

Is Grandma feeling any better?

SOMETHING HORRIFIC HAPPENED AFTER DINNER ON Friday. Nanda was having a bath, and I was reading in my room when Dad came in and sat on the end of my bed.

He cleared his throat.

He didn't look mad, and I couldn't think of anything I'd done wrong.

He crossed his legs. Then uncrossed them. Then cleared his throat again.

"I think there are lozenges under the sink," I said.

"Speaking of the sink . . ." he said. "When I was in the bathroom yesterday, I noticed you had some . . . products . . . out."

I had no idea what he was talking about.

"With your mom gone . . . usually she would talk to you about this . . . you probably know from school . . ."

I put my book down and sat up on my bed so I could be ready to call 9-1-1 if Dad was having a stroke or a nervous breakdown or some sort of early dementia.

"When a girl reaches puberty, there are certain changes in her body . . ."

Red flashing lights and alarm bells went off in my brain. "Dad!!"

"It can be hard to talk about, but there's no need to be embarrassed if . . ."

Nanda's maxi-pad wrappers. All over the bathroom floor. Dad must have found them and thought—

"Dad! Stop! Stop talking! Stop talking right now!" I clapped my hands over my ears and closed my eyes.

It didn't work.

"If you want, we can get your mom on the phone again . . ."

"They weren't mine!"

I gave up on the ear-blocking technique. Instead, I stood up and tried to push him off my bed and out of my room.

"Not yours?"

I shook my head firmly.

Though he still looked confused, he raised his arms in surrender and allowed himself to be evicted.

"I don't want to ever, ever talk to you about this again. Understood?"

He nodded. "Understood."

Then I closed the door in his face.

I decided to never leave my room again.

To: cleocleobear@gmail.com
From: myamyapapaya1@gmail.com
Subject: Our continuing friendship

I was waiting for you to call me and you didn't, probably because you're texting or growing dragons. You're going to forget all about me now that you live in cell phone–land. Don't talk about anything important without me! And if anyone texts you anything interesting, call me right away.

Also, we have to plan for our club meeting on Monday. Call me, call me! Or email. Or chip some hieroglyphics into a stone and push it to my doorstep. My house is crazy and you're my only link to the wider world . . .

CLEO AND I ARE BEST FRIENDS BECAUSE OUR MINDS work the same way. For example, when Ms. Martinson asked us what technology had made the biggest difference in human history, Cleo and I said "cell phone" at *exactly* the same time. It was as if our brains were formed on the same planet.

Nanda's brain, on the other hand, was formed on Pluto and came hurtling through outer space until it landed in Vancouver. It's my theory that on its way through space, her brain received high doses of radiation, making her a complete mutant.

On Saturday morning, I walked out the front door and straight into a net of multicolored wool.

"Nanda!"

It was like being caught in a giant spiderweb. The more I struggled, the more wool wrapped itself around my limbs.

"You're wrecking them!" Nanda shrieked, her head appearing in the second-floor window above me. "You're wrecking my zip lines!"

"I'm trying to go outside!"

"Stop pulling them!"

"Get me out!"

Things continued that way until Dad appeared at another upstairs window, with his hair sticking up in the back like a rooster's tail. He said our neighbors were going to move away if we kept shouting like lunatics at nine on a Saturday morning, and where did I think I was going anyway?

So this was all *my* fault?

Nanda had covered half the house in webs of wool, making zip lines for her collection of army men, and I was the one in trouble for trying to use the front door. Sometimes I wished I could snap my fingers and a judge and jury would appear beside me to give an objective ruling.

"Mya?" Dad waited, eyebrows raised.

"I was going to Cleo's. Just for a while." I'd left him a note on the kitchen table. It was important that I get out of the house early that morning because if I didn't . . .

"I need you to rake the leaves, and don't forget lunch with Auntie Winnie."

Why didn't he just throw a boulder out the window and spatter my guts on the sidewalk?

"Can't Nanda rake the leaves?" My sister was obviously in need of productive activity.

"She's going to clean her room."

Here was another example of why I needed a magically materializing judge. My side of our room was spotless. Did I get credit for this? NO! I got sent outside to rake masses of leaves, which were half from the neighbors' trees anyway and sometimes had disgusting bugs in them. Nanda got to stay inside and tidy her ridiculous stuffed animals.

I never found time to visit Cleo. Instead, I stayed and taste-tested all the food Auntie Winnie brought with her, which wasn't so bad, I guess.

I love food from Myanmar—Aunt Winnie is a great cook. My favorite dish is called Ohn No Kauk Swe. You pronounce it "oh-no-cow-sway." It's chicken and coconut sauce poured over noodles. There are lots of other good meals too.

This week, Auntie Winnie had brought us beef curry and vegetable lentil curry. These would probably save us from having to eat burnt broccoli until at least Wednesday.

However, there are two universal truths about food from Myanmar. The curries are delicious, spicy and a little bit sweet. The desserts, on the other hand, are slimy squares made with things like sesame seeds, which are NOT reasonable dessert ingredients.

Along with her curries, Auntie Winnie brought us mango pudding that she'd cooked herself. It jiggled. It jiggled the way Principal Richards's arms do when she waves her hands around during assembly.

"I should have been on a cooking show," Auntie Winnie said, as she put a big plop of the stuff onto my plate. "I would have called it *Winnie Cooks the Winning Dish*."

"*Winning with Winnie!*" Nanda said, her mouth already full because to my sister, any sugar was good sugar.

"You've certainly fed us well," Dad said, though I noticed he wasn't exactly gobbling up his serving.

Auntie Winnie is six years older than my mom. She has frizzy hair and a large mole on the left side of her nose. I don't want to be mean, but she doesn't exactly look like a glamorous TV chef. In reality, she works at an insurance office. She'd just started a job at a new company, which was why she couldn't go to Myanmar and take care of Grandma.

The pudding wouldn't have done well on TV either. It looked like slime mold. I had to pretend to eat it, scooping tiny spoonfuls into my mouth. It wasn't easy to hold my breath, smile and say "yum" at the same time.

Finally, Auntie Winnie got up to use the bathroom. As soon as she was gone, Dad sent Nanda to get napkins from the pantry. Then he picked one of Mom's ferns right out of its pot, slid our puddings into the hole and replaced the fern.

"Filed them," he said.

When Nanda and Auntie Winnie came back, we rubbed our tummies as if we'd turned into Buddhas.

It was pretty awesome. Dad might not have been the best cook, but he did have some useful life skills.

To: p.lwyn@hotmail.com
From: myamyapapaya1@gmail.com
Subject: Snakes and Ladders

Thanks for the postcards! That reclining Buddha is amaZING! He's HUGE! How did people hundreds of years ago even build something so big? I mean, I'm sure ladders were invented, but can you imagine carving that guy with no power tools? We should travel back in time and sell electric saws. We would be billionaires!

Nanda loved her giant python postcard too. She's been showing it to the entire universe and telling everyone the story about the monk who was reincarnated as a snake.

BTW, power tools. Dad will need to use one on his hair soon. I am withholding comment, because I'm diplomatic, but if he's not careful, he's going to be born again as a hedgehog. Just saying.

Please kiss Grandma for me, and take lots of pictures, and don't get eaten by pythons.

xoxoxoxoxoxoxoxoxoxoxoxo
Mya

EVERY MONDAY AT LUNCH, WE HAD A "KIDS FOR SOCIAL Justice" meeting. Cleo and I started the club in sixth grade, after Mom told me about the government in Myanmar imprisoning a newspaper editor named U Win Tin. She told me his story on EXACTLY the same day Cleo finished *I Am Malala*. (See what I mean about Cleo and me being from the same planet? We are seriously synchronized.)

Until a few years ago, Myanmar was ruled by the military. U Win Tin believed it should be a democracy instead and that everyone should be allowed to vote in elections. The military didn't like that idea. They threw him in jail. Not just for six weeks to teach him a lesson either. He was there for NINETEEN YEARS. They kept him in a dog kennel with no bed and they didn't give him enough food. But as soon as he was released, even though he was ancient by that time, he went right back to writing about democracy and visiting the families of political prisoners and basically being awesome.

Malala was a girl who went to school in Pakistan, where lots of people believe girls shouldn't go to school. Which at first I thought was a fantastic idea, until I figured out that instead of going to class, they were supposed to stay home and sweep the house and cook eggplants all day. I don't even like eggplants.

Malala wrote essays about school being a good thing, then people made a documentary about her, and then some guy SHOT HER IN THE HEAD! How crazy is that? But just like U Win Tin (except younger and with much less ear hair), she got right back to work. She popped out of her hospital bed and started giving talks about how *obviously* girls should go to school. Then she won the Nobel Peace Prize.

I told Cleo about U Win Tin and she told me about Malala, in a conversation that went like this:

ME: He was tortured, and can you imagine prison in Myanmar? And—

CLEO: —then she was flown to England for surgery—

ME: Mom says hardly anyone outside Myanmar has even heard of him—

CLEO: —her dad believed in education for girls too . . .

At the end of all that, Kids for Social Justice was born. Cleo and I were determined to win Nobel prizes, like Malala, except without getting shot, or sleeping in dog kennels either.

At first, KSJ was just the two of us, but we made posters and gave presentations in all our classes. By seventh grade, there were about twelve kids. Some weeks, Cleo and I chose an issue and we all wrote letters to politicians. Other weeks, when we didn't want to horrify everyone with the world's ridiculously MAJOR problems, we created art pieces and mailed those instead. (That was Mom's idea.)

Unfortunately, thanks to a *certain someone* not calling me back (let's just say her name rhymed with "Bleo"), we hadn't picked a subject for Monday's meeting.

"Where were you?" I asked her, as soon as we met on the sidewalk that morning. Nanda was already way ahead of me.

She turned and waved as she beetled into her schoolyard.

"What do you mean?" Cleo asked.

"I left you two messages, and you never called back. We have to talk about KSJ."

She wrinkled her nose. "Sorry. I got busy."

"I'm pretty sure you have to return your best friend's phone messages in order to one day win a Nobel Peace Prize." Otherwise you weren't being a good communicator, which wouldn't be helpful for international relations either.

"Okay, okay." Cleo flapped her hands. "I'm sorry. What do we need to do?"

"Choose a subject!"

But the bell rang as soon as we passed the school fence, which meant we had no time AT ALL to properly discuss the issue.

"Can we just skip it this week?" Cleo asked. "I told Drew I would show him how to use emojis."

I stopped dead at the main door. "You told him *what*?"

"Emojis," she said. "He doesn't know how to use emojis."

"How did this happen?"

"Well, he hasn't had his phone very long." She grabbed my sleeve and tugged me toward the classroom, because my feet had stopped working.

"Not the emojis. How did you end up talking to Drew on the weekend?"

"JoJo sent me a list of everyone's cell number. When I saw him on the list, I thought I should apologize. You know, for the water bottle thing."

JoJo was the first person in our grade to get a phone, and also the first to get boobs, which I assumed was coincidental.

By the time I digested Cleo's story, our homeroom teacher was taking attendance.

"So can we skip the meeting?" Cleo whispered.

"No!"

"Well, who are we going to write about then?"

"I'll figure it out," I said.

"And what about . . . ?" Cleo tilted her head in Drew's direction.

"*You* figure it out."

If Cleo couldn't understand that social justice issues outweighed emojis, I wasn't about to explain.

Meeting Minutes
Kids for Social Justice
September 25

1. Report on violence in Myanmar (Mya Parsons)
   - The Rohingya are a Muslim minority in Myanmar. They've been persecuted by the government basically forever. A few of them revolted. In response, the military decided, "Kill them all! Burn their villages!"
   - According to UN reports, more than 400,000 Rohingya refugees have crossed the border from Myanmar to Bangladesh as of this month.

2. Discussion of response to Rohingya situation
   - Cleo moves that Kids for Social Justice raise money for the Rohingya children in refugee camps. Motion seconded by Matthew. Approved unanimously.
   - Bake sale to be held on Friday, October 6th.
3. Be it resolved that Kids for Social Justice is dedicated to solving the refugee crisis!

"EYES ON ME, CLASS," MS. MARTINSON SAID ON THE last Tuesday in September. She clasped her hands in front of her, a sign she was about to announce a new project.

Everyone went silent. We'd had Ms. Martinson for English in sixth grade too. Sometimes her project ideas were good, and sometimes they were not so good.

"We are going to launch an exciting unit of inquiry. You'll be researching different ways that people have communicated throughout history."

"Like email?" JoJo said.

"Exactly. JoJo, perhaps you and your partner can write about that."

At the word *partner*, Cleo and I immediately linked arms, even though Cleo'd spent all of Monday's KSJ meeting whispering with Drew, so I technically wasn't speaking to her.

"Who can name another way?" Ms. Martinson asked.

Both Cleo and I shot our hands into the air, Cleo practically bouncing out of her seat.

"Phone," she said, when Ms. Martinson called on her.

"Cell phone," I clarified.

"That's a good contemporary example, girls."

"We *have* to do the cell phone," Cleo whispered to me.

"Definitely."

Ms. Martinson was still explaining the rules. ". . . A written report, as well as a presentation for the class. You can get creative with these. Create slide shows, design posters . . . one of my groups last year even filmed a music video."

Ian waved his hand in the air as if he was going to explode if Ms. Martinson didn't acknowledge him.

"Yes, Ian?"

"Can we do smoke signals?"

"Yes."

"And use real fire?"

"No."

There was a collective groan from the boys, because they were collective idiots.

"I have some poster board here, and I've booked us several sessions in the computer lab. You may also wish to bring materials from home. We're going to be working on these projects over the next several weeks." Then Ms. Martinson showed us her samples from last year, which were mildly impressive but nothing compared to what Cleo and I could create together.

"We'll need to have some evening sessions," I whispered to Cleo.

"With chocolate," she said.

"Maybe Dad will buy us a frozen cake."

When we'd had a sleepover the year before to work on a science project, the two of us finished an entire half-thawed chocolate cake, eating it straight from the box with our forks. It was the most delicious thing I'd ever tasted, and we got TONS done because we couldn't sleep anyways.

Everyone was already whispering, but Ms. Martinson held up her hand. "I've assigned partners. I suggest you start by researching possible topics."

This time, there was a collective groan from the girls, and Cleo and I stared at each other as if we'd been stabbed. Whenever Ms. Martinson chose our partners, it was because she was trying to kill us. I was pretty sure it was a torture technique that teachers learned in college.

She quickly reeled off pairs of names: JoJo and Rahul, Simon and Ella B. This was sounding especially bad. Sure enough, when she reached our corner of the classroom, Cleo and Drew.

I knew what was coming next. I almost crawled beneath my desk.

"Mya and Ian, you'll be working together."

What had I ever done to make Ms. Martinson hate me? I scowled at Ian. He scowled back, which was ridiculous, because he'd obviously gotten the better deal.

"Go ahead and start your planning," Ms. Martinson said. "At the end of the week, you'll need to hand in the name of your communication style and a summary of your ideas."

Ian and I stared at each other. Beside us, Cleo and Drew had already bent their heads together, whispering. I transferred my glare to Cleo, but she didn't notice.

Ms. Martinson tapped her fingers on my desk. "Share some ideas with your partner," she said.

"World War II codes," Ian said. Then he made bomb sound effects.

"No."

"How are we supposed to agree on something?"

"Cell phones!" Did he not listen, ever?

"No way," he said.

"What?"

"Too boring."

I was flabbergasted. Flabber. Gasted.

Ms. Martinson was still standing beside us. "I'm sure you can find a topic that's mutually acceptable," she said. Which is another thing she must have learned in teacher's college. How to sound helpful without being any help at all.

To: cleocleobear@gmail.com
From: myamyapapaya1@gmail.com
Subject: Happy No Kabooms Day!

I spent my screen time on the UN website tonight, and guess what? September 26th is the International Day for the Total Elimination of Nuclear Weapons. Not just elimination either. TOTAL elimination. Next year we'll have to have cake at KSJ to celebrate the idea.

Also, I read the careers page of the website. Check this out:

> *Does making a difference motivate you? Are you selfless*
> *and driven to be a part of a bigger purpose in the service*
> *of humanity? And, are hope and strength of character*
> *attributes that guide your zeal to make a difference in a*
> *complex world?*

Yes, yes and yes!! When I'm a diplomat and you're a famous
fashion designer, we should share a European apartment. A
pied-à-terre. I can't wait!

To: p.lwyn@hotmail.com
From: myamyapapaya1@gmail.com
Subject: Big changes

Dear Mom,
I don't know what Dad's talking about, or why he's talking about
it to you when you're in MYANMAR! Please never, ever type the
word *menstruation* again. Why did they even have to name it that?
I think old-man doctor-scientists came up with the weirdest,
ugliest word they could. Why didn't they call it "the mense" or
"the big stru" or . . . never mind. Those are just as bad. But there
must have been SOME other option.

Argh! Now you have ME talking about it, and I think we
just agreed not to do that, ever, so let's consider the matter
settled.

When you and Grandma are ready to come home, can you bring me some tamarind candies? The kind with squiggly writing on the wrappers? I want to pass them out to my class. Well, to *most* of my class.

Love and xoxoxoxoxoxoxoxoxoxoxoxo,
Mya

AT BREAKFAST ON WEDNESDAY (CINNAMON STRUDELS were Dad's latest find), I brought up THE subject. Okay, not THE subject as in my nonexistent period, but THE subject as in the actual important part of my transition to adulthood.

"Cleo loves her new cell phone," I said.

"They should put more icing on these strudels," Nanda said.

Dad said nothing. He had his head in the fridge trying to find something for our lunches. It was as if he'd suddenly gone deaf.

"Are you listening?"

"Dad, don't forget it's orange day at school. I have to take orange things," Nanda said. Which explained her outfit. It defied description. Though "rotting pumpkin" would have been appropriate.

"What?" Dad said.

"Orange things," Nanda said.

"Her cell phone," I said at the same time.

Dad looked a little tired. Since we'd all been eating a LOT of carbohydrates since Mom left, I suggested that he try the paleo diet, which Cleo's mom was doing. She was only eating things that had existed since the Stone Age.

Dad made a little growling noise in the back of his throat, so I waited until he'd dealt with Nanda's orange needs.

"Okay, I have canned mandarins, a bag of Doritos, and I'll beep-semble you a cheese sandwich. Will that do?"

Nanda nodded happily.

Finally, once Dad was sitting down, I asked about getting my own phone. I used my most reasonable manner. Even though my dad is an environmental lawyer, which sounds all warm and fuzzy, he's still a lawyer. He appreciates logic.

He said no, no way and never.

"What if everyone in my class had a cell phone? Then could I have one?"

Dad sighed. "Every single person?"

"Every single one."

"If everyone had a phone . . . every single other person . . ." He paused for a long time. "Then you'd be the only person without one," he said finally.

He and Nanda giggled as if he were the funniest guy in history. Just wait until *she* is in seventh grade and wants her own phone. Then she'll be sorry.

Also, it was very cruel of a father to crush his daughter's dreams. I thought it showed a blatant disregard for my feelings.

BAKE SALE!

Friday, October 6th

SAVE THE ROHINGYA
REFUGEES IN BANGLADESH!

COOKIES! CAKES! MORE!

KSJ CLUB

WE HAD A SPECIAL RECESS MEETING OF KSJ ON THURSDAY
to make posters for the bake sale, and we decided to make
more at our Monday meeting. This sale would be amaZING!
Although Cleo said we should try to give our dishes international flair, so I needed to think of a Myanmar-ish dessert
that was somewhat edible.

I supposed this would be good practice for my future
with the United Nations, which would often involve chal-
lenges. I'd have even more dedication than I needed, because
I'd been preparing since I was nine.

On our trip to Myanmar that year, we spent a whole
afternoon driving from one old person's house to the next.
At every stop, Nanda and I knelt on the floor and smiled
while Mom and Dad drank tea, chatted and gave out envelopes of money. The envelopes were *gah dau*, signs of
respect, Mom said, in between telling us that (a) she didn't
care if our knees had bamboo-mat patterns on them and
(b) we'd better be polite or else.

Our final stop was at Daw Gyi's house. She was the thin-
nest and most wrinkled of all the great-aunts. When she
smiled, there was a black hole where her front teeth should
have been.

As she shuffled toward us, I decided I was going to die
of boredom and overpoliteness. I'd collapse right there in
Daw Gyi's living room, into a sweaty, mosquito-bitten lump.

Then Mom would be sorry.

"It's so wonderful to meet you, Mya," Daw Gyi said, taking both my hands in hers.

I almost fell over for completely different reasons. Daw Gyi *looked* like a traditional auntie, but she *talked* like someone on the news, with the tiniest hint of a British accent.

"Have a little look in the kitchen," she told Nanda and me.

On the table were (a) shortbread cookies in a fancy tin and (b) all sorts of puzzles. There were normal Rubik's Cubes and triangle-shaped versions, carved wooden logic puzzles, and balanced towers of blocks. At home, the table might not have been so appealing, but after an eternity of relative visits, Nanda and I thought we'd found Disneyland.

After she'd chatted with my parents, Daw Gyi joined us. She took a Rubik's Cube from my hands, pointed to my watch and said, "Time me."

Three minutes, twenty-three seconds.

"Oh dear. I'm a tad rusty," she said.

Then it was time to go.

In the car on the way back to the guesthouse, Mom said Daw Gyi had once worked for the United Nations and had traveled all around the world. Some of her puzzles were from Africa, Mom said.

"Can we go back and see her?" I asked.

"One day," Mom said.

As it turned out, we couldn't. Daw Gyi died a year later. But by that time, I'd already done an entire school project on the United Nations and I had my career plan all mapped out. I would have totally figured out the Rubik's Cube too, if Nanda hadn't broken mine.

To: p.lwyn@hotmail.com
From: myamyapapaya1@gmail.com
Subject: My request

Dear Mom,

I heard Dad talking to you on the phone about my cell request, and I did not appreciate his laughter. I do not think it was a diplomatic response.

I hope you will intervene on my behalf, as obviously a cell phone will be helpful in keeping us safe while you're away. Cleo is using her phone to communicate about a school project, which I think is very mature and responsible, even though her partner is Drew, who is neither of those things.

PS There *are* chocolate strudels, and Dad bought some, but they are horrible. They don't taste at all like real chocolate. Not even Nanda could eat them.

PPS Nanda just got home from soccer and wants me to tell you that she scored three goals in their scrimmage.

PPPS Please tell Dad to get a haircut. That sticky-up tuft on the back of his head is now HUGE, and it will be extraordinarily embarrassing if my friends see it.

WE WERE SUPPOSED TO CHOOSE A TOPIC FOR OUR project within a week, and Ms. Martinson told us to brainstorm as many ideas as possible over the weekend. These were some of my thoughts:

Ways to Avoid Working with Ian

- Fake a rare genetic disease.
- Catch bubonic plague.
- Request to visit the school counselor between 2 and 3 p.m. daily.
- Lock myself in the bathroom and refuse to come out, like Ella C. did in second grade.
- Stage my own death. (Request that Cleo sing at my funeral. Ask Dad to buy me a white dress so I could be properly, angelically attired in the casket.)

Cleo once told me about a puffer-fish poison that could lower the heart rate so much you were declared dead. She said one guy in Japan woke up in the morgue!

That would totally get me out of this assignment. Maybe I should have watched Nanda's zombie show more carefully.

I tried a second brainstorming round, but it turned into a whole page of "Cell Phone" written in different colors. How could I not write about the most advanced form of communication when it was the most important subject in my life? I even looked up the inventor of the cell phone. His name was Martin Cooper, but there was a reason no one had ever heard of him. He was SO boring. He worked for Motorola and the company gave him about $100 million to develop his invention. Seriously? I could invent *anything* if I had $100 million.

I considered expanding our topic to include *all* phones, because I also looked up Alexander Graham Bell. His wife and his mom were deaf, so he was studying sound waves to try to help them and that's when he discovered telephone technology. *Ultra-romantico*, as Cleo would say. Also, Bell had a beep-sistant named Watson, just like Sherlock Holmes.

Plus this: another inventor was researching sound transmission AT THE SAME TIME. And that guy—the nemesis of Alexander Graham Bell—filed for a patent on his device AT THE SAME TIME, and it was a race to see who would get to be the real inventor. Bell won.

Ian and I were going to win too, if Cleo and Drew submitted their own phone proposal. Because ours would be better and because now I'd covered another sheet of paper with "Cell Phone" and "Telephone" and "Alexander Graham Bell" in a lot of different colors AND sizes, so we already had a title page practically finished. How could Ms. Martinson say no?

PART II

THREE WEEKS WITHOUT MOM

D AD ASKED ME TO TIDY THE LIVING ROOM BEFORE bed. Mostly, this meant ferrying a lot of plates and cups into the kitchen, recycling newspapers and carrying some of Nanda's toxic-waste soccer clothes to our laundry bin. For extra brownie points, I dusted the coffee table. I was feeling quite impressed with myself, until I noticed the shrine.

In one corner of our living room, Mom has a tall rose-wood cabinet. That's her shrine. A foldout shelf in the middle holds a collection of bells, a carved wooden statue of Buddha and photos of Shwedagon Pagoda, a gold temple in Myanmar. There are small bowls at the front of the shelf where Mom places offerings each morning.

Two small problems: (a) Buddha didn't actually eat those offerings, and (b) Mom had been away for three weeks, which meant moldy rice. Seriously moldy rice.

I picked up the bowls one at a time and ferried them to the kitchen at arm's length, holding my nose with my other hand so I wouldn't breathe spores. Then I dumped the green and fuzzy contents in the compost bin, hand-washed the bowls and replaced them on the shrine.

Before bed, Dad gave me a dollar because he said I'd done such a good job on the living room. This was unexpected, but not exactly a stretch on his wallet.

I fell asleep wondering if Buddha might be more generous.

MS. MARTINSON SAID NO, DESPITE MY TITLE PAGE. She said Cleo and Drew had submitted early, ON FRIDAY. They were already planning their presentation about the evolution of the telephone from Alexander Graham Bell until today, and she didn't want two groups studying the same thing "when there are so many innovative forms to discover."

I was crushed. I wanted to innovate myself right back to bed.

"We can't do our project about phones. And Ms. Martinson says we have to choose a topic by Thursday at the absolute latest," I told Ian.

The news didn't seem to bother him. He and Drew had removed the erasers from the backs of their pencils and were flicking them across their desks, trying to score in folded paper goals. Which completely explained the whole boy/girl literacy rate difference, because we were supposed to be practicing our spelling.

Though I wasn't practicing my spelling either. I was too busy feeling fatally betrayed by my best friend.

"I can't believe you handed in your proposal on Friday!"

I hissed to Cleo, as soon as Ms. Martinson stepped out of the room.

"I'm sorry," Cleo said. "We were finished early. I didn't think it would matter." She gave me her wide-eyed, innocent look, but I fought against it.

"I would have known you'd handed it in if you'd called me back on Saturday, which you didn't."

"My mom made me go to a digital literacy presentation. It was terrible."

"A what?"

"A two-hour lecture on how not to send a photo of your boobs to anyone, because that person might email someone else and then post your boobs on the Internet, and you'll get harassed by creepy stranger creepy-creeps, and before you know it you'll be calling suicide hotlines, all because your mom bought you a phone."

By this time Ian and Drew had paused their eraser-hockey and were staring at us, and Ms. Martinson had returned to the room and was standing at the door, staring at us too. Saying "boobs" out loud in a seventh-grade classroom was like saying "bomb" in an airport.

Ms. Martinson shook her head and got her feet moving again. "Spelling, girls," she said.

"Come over after school on Wednesday," Cleo whispered.

I nodded, and that was the end of the Alexander Graham Bell conflict, except that Ian and I still had no subject for our project. And since I really didn't want to talk to him about it, I couldn't see how we were going to come up with one.

SENYINMAKIN, AKA SEMI-EDIBLE SQUARES

(Semolina is apparently a weird kind of wheat flour. I can't believe Mom actually had some in the cupboard. Also, if you get distracted and forget to stir the semolina, and it gets burned instead of toasted, you should NOT—I repeat, NOT—continue with the recipe, because the whole thing will turn into a lump of ashes and your dad will say, "What smells like burnt toast?" and your sister will laugh hysterically, and you will be inclined to cry at the complete failure of your bake sale dreams.)

2¼ cups semolina
½ cup vegetable oil
2½ cups coconut milk
2½ cups sugar
2 teaspoons salt
2 eggs
½ cup raisins

Heat oven to 400°F. Grease a 9-inch round cake pan. Heat semolina on medium-high in a large pot, stirring until it's lightly toasted.

Add oil, coconut milk, sugar, salt, eggs and 2½ cups water. Continue to cook and stir until the mixture comes away from the side of the pot, which seems to take forever and you'll think your arm is going to fall off, but it's actually about 10 more minutes. Add raisins. Spread the goo in the cake pan and then bake for 45 minutes.

MOM CALLED ON TUESDAY NIGHT. I GRABBED THE PHONE first, and I was going to ask her for project ideas, but there was no time. I hadn't even finished talking about my bake sale issues, my personal cell-phone needs and Dad's *truly horrific* hair, when she said the international phone lines were bad and I was breaking up. Then she talked to Nanda for ten minutes all about the new skateboarding park opening near our house.

Dad promised Nanda that she could try skateboarding as long as she wore safety gear. Apparently, he'd always wanted to skateboard, so everything about it was wonderful. But he never needed a cell phone when he was a kid (because: dark ages), so phones were evil.

Did anyone else in my family see the injustice here?

That would be no.

I was the *only* one who made decisions based on reason.

I talked about this with Mr. Gupta, the school counselor. I managed to get an appointment at exactly 2:10 p.m. on Wednesday.

"So you feel your family members aren't really listening?" he asked.

"I *know* they're not listening."

Even though I was only in his office to avoid brainstorming with Ian, Mr. Gupta actually had good advice. He said that sometimes, in a busy household, it can be difficult for people to connect on a deeper level. He suggested I write a letter. According to Mr. Gupta, that would allow me to clarify my own thoughts while also communicating clearly with Dad.

He said some other stuff about me learning to listen in return, empathy, etc., etc., but I wasn't concentrating anymore.

"Do you think I could write my letter in your office?" I asked. "You've really achieved a nice atmosphere here."

He said yes, and that settled the matter.

Dear Dad,

I'm writing to request that I be allowed a cell phone.

Now that I am walking Nanda to school and picking her up on my way home, a cell phone will allow me to contact you immediately in case of an emergency. It will also allow *you* to contact *me*, should you be anxious about my safety at any time.

Of the seventeen girls in my class, nine have cell phones and six others say they're getting phones absolutely, for sure, before the end of seventh grade. Of the nine who already own them, all nine say their devices significantly add to their safety. Also, three have phones with leopard-print cases which, I may say, seem like they would make phones much more difficult to misplace. Not that I would ever lose my phone.

I appreciate your consideration of this important matter.

Sincerely,

Mya Parsons

Mya Parsons
Your loving and responsible daughter

I SHOWED CLEO MY LETTER ONCE WE WERE AT HER house eating our after-school snack, which was cauliflower popcorn. Cauliflower popcorn was apparently part of her mom's new paleo craze. It was cauliflower cut into tiny pieces, sprinkled with salt and roasted. I was *so* happy Dad hadn't taken my advice about the paleo diet, because this stuff tasted horrible and not at all like popcorn, unless maybe you squinted your eyes until your vision turned blurry and didn't actually eat anything.

"Are you supposed to serve this when it's hot, maybe?"

"It's perfect," Cleo said. But she was talking about my letter, not the snack.

"Do you think it will work?"

"Definitely." The wide-eyed look again. If I had eyes like Cleo's, I would have had a cell phone years ago.

Once she put the cauliflower back in the fridge and found some old Easter candy for us in the bottom of her closet, we flopped onto her bed.

"Would you rather eat only cauliflower for the rest of your life, or would you rather drink only grapefruit juice, forever?" she asked. Cleo and I both hated grapefruit juice, which was another indicator we may have been twins separated at birth.

"Ugh. Neither."

"You have to choose one. That's the rule."

"Cauliflower."

"Agreed."

My turn. "Would you rather go to school for a year with

your underwear outside your clothes or keep your head shaved for the rest of your life?"

"What kind of underwear?" she asked.

"Any kind."

"Panties and bra?"

As if Cleo wore a bra. "Sports bra."

"I'd choose underwear, then."

"I'd shave my head," I said.

"You would not!"

"I could get a wig. You can't hide your underwear."

"You can't get a wig," she protested. "That's cheating."

"I never said you couldn't wear wigs."

"Fine. Would you rather kiss Ian Winters or Drew Powell?" she asked.

"Gross!" I leaned over the edge of the bed so I could pretend to puke my guts out on the floor.

"If you *had* to choose," she said.

Cleo opened her eyes wide at me, but I hesitated. Was I supposed to pick Drew, and thus agree with her that he was cute, or was I supposed to pick Ian, so she could have Drew all to herself?

"You have to choose one. That's the rule," she said.

Stupid rule. "Do I get disinfectant mouthwash afterward?"

"As much as you want."

"Ian, then."

Cleo squealed. "I knew it! This is so perfect! You like Ian and I like Drew!" She hugged her pillow to her stomach and bounced up and down on the mattress.

I considered crawling under the bed.

"I do NOT like Ian," I said.

"You already admitted it," she said. "And he's a nice guy. Not as cute as Drew, but nice. Have you noticed that Drew's eyes have light brown specks inside them?"

"Do we have to talk about this? Can we go back to talking about cell phones?"

Cleo patted me on the back as if I were a toddler and she was the responsible adult in the room. "Okay." Then she whispered, "He does have really cute eyes."

"Argh!" I squished a pillow over my head.

After a minute, Cleo lifted the corner. "I'm ready to talk about cell phones now," she promised. "You know what you should say after you give your dad the letter? You should talk more about how you're taking care of Nanda a lot, with your mom away. Because that's a big responsibility, showing that you're . . ."

Her words trailed off because I'd bolted upright. My breath had frozen in my chest.

"What's —"

"Nanda! I forgot to pick up Nanda!" I leapt off her bed and ran downstairs.

I was hopping toward Cleo's entranceway, pulling on my second shoe as I went, when her mom opened the door.

"Mya," she said. "What a nice surprise!"

"Got to go! Late to pick up my sister!" About two hours late. It was already getting dark. I pictured Nanda sitting on the steps of the school, alone.

"Let me give you a ride," Cleo's mom said.

"That's okay! Thanks, though." I ducked past her and sprinted down the street. I didn't need Cleo's mom with me when I found my sister waiting, with snot dripping from her chin and the streetlights flicking on around her.

Cleo only lived a few blocks away, so it didn't take me long to get to Nanda's school.

She wasn't there.

The steps were empty. I tried the front doors, but they were locked.

Be okay. Be okay. Please be okay. The words circled in my brain, and I wasn't sure if they were for Nanda or for me.

I had lost my sister. How was I going to explain this? I may as well give up all hope of a cell phone. I'd probably be placed in foster care. And what if Nanda had been picked up by some psychopathic kidnapper in a white panel van with tinted windows? Maybe that old guy who walked his golden retriever every afternoon only looked innocent but was actually a mass murderer with a torture chamber in his basement and now he had my sister.

I couldn't breathe properly. My lungs burning, I sprinted toward home. The lights were on. Which meant either Nanda was there, safe, or Dad was organizing search parties for both of us. I flung open the front door —

"Nanda!"

"Hey," she said. She was eating toast in front of the TV. On the screen, doctors were performing open-heart surgery. Even in my oxygen-deprived state, I could see that the jam on her toast exactly matched the blood.

Black static fuzzed at the edges of my vision. I felt myself swaying. I had to lean over, put my hands on my knees, and concentrate on sucking in some proper breaths. When the dizziness passed and I looked up, Nanda's eyes were still glued to the operation.

I stepped between her and the TV. "How did you get home?"

"Ian's mom gave me a ride."

"Ian who?"

"Ian in your class. His little brother goes to my school, and you weren't there, so I asked them for a ride. Did you know Ian has a skateboard? And he wants to be a beep-stronaut when he grows up?"

I felt sick again. "You can't ask for rides from strangers!"

"But you weren't there," she said. "And they're not strangers. Can you move? You're blocking everything."

I turned off the TV, ignoring her protests. Then I collapsed onto the couch beside her. "Seriously, this is important. You can't ask people for rides."

She shrugged. "Ian's nice. They have video screens right inside their van. They flip down from the roof."

I considered strangling her.

Then she looked up at me. "Where were you? You were supposed to get me."

If my previous panic felt like a storm swirling inside me, this felt as if I'd been crushed by a telephone pole. I opened my mouth and closed it a few times as I tried to figure out a reasonable explanation. I couldn't think of anything.

"I messed up."

Nanda's eyes widened.

"Sorry."

Eventually, she nodded. "Can I turn my show back on?"

"Can you promise not to take rides from other people?"

"Can you promise not to forget me?" she asked.

"Deal."

But there was one more thing to settle.

"If I don't tell Dad about the ride, can you not tell him I was late?"

"Deal," she said.

It seemed as if we were not from different planets after all.

To: cleocleobear@gmail.com

From: myamyapapaya1@gmail.com

Subject: AHHHHHHHHHHHH! Again!!!

So, I found my sister. She was at home because she asked for a ride from a potential murderer, who turned out to be Ian's mom, but STILL.

It gets worse. I gave my dad the letter, as we discussed. He read it while we were eating our pizza. But he folded it up afterward and said, "We'll talk about this once you've proven you can show a greater sense of responsibility." Then he tilted his head toward my sister.

Because NANDA TOLD ON ME. Even after we made a deal. We specifically agreed not to mention the forgotten pick-up and kidnapper ride-taking issues, then she went and RATTED!

I have been betrayed by my own sister, and my hopes of joining the twenty-first century have met a tragic end. I'll see you at school tomorrow if I'm not bedridden, nursing my broken spirit.

xoxoxoxoxoxoxoxoxoxoxoxoxo

M.

To: p.lwyn@hotmail.com
From: myamyapapaya1@gmail.com
Subject: Dolphin healing vibes

Dear Mom,

We had a special presentation from aquarium volunteers at school today. Did you know that dolphins only rest half their brains at one time, so the other half can keep them swimming and breathing? I was thinking I should suggest this to Dad, since he seems to have trouble keeping up around here sometimes. And maybe if Grandma could train her brain for dolphin half-sleep, she would heal more quickly, because did you also know that when you sleep, your brain releases hormones that tell your body to rebuild itself?

The presentation took a big chunk of our morning. In the afternoon, we worked on our communications projects. I would be interested IF I didn't have to work with the world's most horrific partner, who refuses to agree on a reasonable topic. I really wanted to research cell phones, but Cleo and Drew chose that topic first. Ian says that's fine because we're going to do something way more original. But I am NOT researching Cro-Magnon cave art and wearing a bone in my hair for the presentation.

We have to pick by tomorrow at the latest. You will be home (hopefully???) before we've done the main part of the project, so you can see our brilliance for yourself.

Love,
Mya

PS In case you hear any stories about me momentarily misplacing something/someone—there are two sides to every situation. And there is usually a perfectly reasonable explanation. I think you should keep an open mind.

DAD BOUGHT A SKATEBOARD FOR NANDA. HE SAID IT would keep her out of trouble. It actually *caused* a lot of trouble. For ME.

Dad made me walk her to the skate park before school on Thursday and she went the whole way—at least a fifteen-minute walk, on public streets—wearing her safety gear. Elbow pads, knee pads, helmet—all bright red, and all strapped onto her body for the highly dangerous journey through our neighborhood. I told her normal skateboarders

60

put on their gear once they are AT the park, but she said that since she was already wearing it at breakfast, it made no sense to take it off.

My sister lived in a world that was so illogical, I couldn't even figure out how to argue with her.

Nanda was also convinced that skateboarders wore zippered hoodies. Unfortunately, the only zippered hoodie she owns is one that Auntie Winnie gave her for her birthday. It's yellow and has ears on the hood and a tail attached at the back.

WHO WOULD WEAR A HOODIE WITH EARS AND A TAIL IN PUBLIC? WITH SAFETY PADS?

My sister. Probably because she knew that I had to walk her to the park and being seen with her would ruin my life.

To: p.lwyn@hotmail.com
From: myamyapapaya1@gmail.com
Subject: Genetics/bake sale

Is there any chance Nanda was adopted?

Also, guess what? We had a Kids for Social Justice bake sale today and we raised $147 for Rohingya kids stuck in the refugee camps in Bangladesh! Principal Richards is going to donate the money to UNICEF for us. You would have been so impressed by our goodies. Cleo's mom made paleo cake pops, which were filled with coconut and chocolate goodness and surprisingly amaZING. Other people brought baklava squares, shortbread, marshmallows dipped in chocolate, Norwegian apple cake, banana bread and more things I can't even remember.

I tried to make a dessert TWICE but it was a complete failure. I ran out of time, and also out of semolina, so Dad drove me to school this morning and we bought oatmeal cookies along the way. I transferred them to a paper plate to make it look as if we'd baked them, which was kind of dishonest but for a good cause. AND they completely sold out so I didn't feel too badly.

If you happen to see any Rohingya kids, tell them help is on the way!

DAD TOOK NANDA TO THE SKATE PARK ON SATURDAY afternoon and I spent a perfect hour watching TV. Then Auntie Winnie turned up with a family dinner à la Myanmar: a huge noodle stir-fry, a beef curry, stuffed peppers and coconut rice. I could have kissed her. Except that Auntie Winnie always wears several layers of makeup and kissing her was like kissing a powder-puff. So I refrained. But I did make appreciative noises while I taste-tested.

"You know," she said, "I could teach you to make these dishes. Wouldn't it surprise your dad if he arrived home from work and you'd cooked dinner?"

I almost snorted a noodle out my nose. "Make a whole dinner?"

Dad would be shocked, not surprised. At his age, that would probably be a stroke risk.

"I'll teach you some one-pot recipes."

Every part of this idea sounded horrible. I'd have to listen to Auntie Winnie give me instructions for an hour, and she (a) treated me like I was six years old and (b) acted as if she was single-handedly saving our family during Mom's absence. Which she sort of was, because her food was keeping us from death by starvation. Still, Mom always said that good deeds should be done with humility. (She usually said this when I told her about my Nobel Peace Prize plans, but if she'd been at home with Auntie Winnie and me, watching me make polite-face until my cheeks hurt, she would know I *deserved* that prize.)

Even if I made it through the actual cooperating-with-Auntie-Winnie part, I'd have to watch other people eat my food. Nanda would probably complain and ask for her usual Toaster Strudel, and then I'd strangle her. I'd be jailed for man-slaughter. Or sisterslaughter. How would that help anyone?

"I don't think so. I have a lot of homework these days," I told Auntie Winnie.

She didn't seem to believe me, so I explained further. "We're working on projects at school. They're supposed to be written reports and oral presentations, but we might make ours a wiki page, or turn it into a slide show. My partner, Ian, is no help at all, so basically I have to take responsibility for the whole thing."

"I see," Auntie Winnie said. She kept staring at me.

"It's a huge drain on my resources." Which was something I'd heard Dad say about his big case at work. It seemed to be effective. (Even though Auntie Winnie conveniently "forgot" one of her recipe cards on the kitchen counter.)

CHEATER'S OHN NO KAUK SWE,
AKA COCONUT NOODLES

(The cheating part is the cream of mushroom soup, which is not exactly a traditional ingredient. But otherwise you have to toast pea powder to thicken the broth, and things get messy and lumpy. Or they could. Theoretically.)

> 1 package vermicelli rice noodles
> ⅓ cup oil
> 1 onion, diced
> 2 cloves garlic, chopped
> 1 tablespoon ginger, grated
> 1 tablespoon Thai red curry paste, mixed with water until smooth
> 2 cups white mushrooms, sliced
> 4 boneless, skinless chicken breasts, diced
> 2 cans coconut milk
> 2 cans cream of mushroom soup
> 1 can chicken broth

Cook vermicelli noodles according to package directions and set aside. Sauté onion in oil over medium heat until softened. Add garlic and ginger, and stir for one minute. Add curry paste and cook until bubbling. Add chicken and stir to coat. Add mushrooms, coconut milk, soup and broth, and bring to a gentle boil. Turn heat to low and simmer for 30 minutes. Serve over noodles. Garnish with cilantro, sliced lime and sliced hard-boiled eggs.

WHILE DAD WAS READING TO NANDA AFTER DINNER, Auntie Winnie sat down across from me at the kitchen table.

"I wanted to discuss something, Mya." She was twisting one of her (many) rings around her finger, but she stopped and folded her hands together.

"Your mom called me. She said you might need someone to talk to. About . . . changes."

Auntie Winnie was already trying to turn me into the family chef. How many other changes could there be?

"Not having children of my own, I've never really thought about how to approach this."

I wouldn't have thought it possible, but she appeared to be flushing.

"And perhaps I think of you and Nanda as younger than you are. Here you're turning into a woman, right before our eyes."

That one word. As soon as she said *woman*, everything became clear. Horrifically clear. It was a good thing I'd already finished my curry.

"Stop! What you think happened? It didn't happen."

I tried getting up from the table, but Auntie Winnie put a hand on my wrist. "These sorts of changes are part of growing up. We all experience them."

Thinking about Auntie Winnie having her period was possibly the grossest moment of my entire existence.

"I didn't experience it!" I blurted. "This whole thing started because Dad saw pads on the bathroom floor, but they were Nanda's!"

"Nanda's?" Auntie Winnie looked shocked.

"Well, Mom's, really."

She stared at me.

"Nanda couldn't find her shin pads."

She still didn't get it.

"For soccer. So she found that box . . ."

Auntie Winnie's lip began to quiver. For a minute, I thought she was about to cry. Then she burst out laughing. I don't think I've ever heard Auntie Winnie laugh so hard. After a while, she put her head down on the table. The noise stopped, but her shoulders kept shaking.

That was the end of our girl talk. In fact, she didn't even say goodbye. She just kept muttering "shin pads" under her breath on her way to the door. Every time she said it, she'd start shaking all over again.

Some people had issues with emotional control.

To: cleocleobear@gmail.com
From: myamyapapaya1@gmail.com
Subject: Your good idea and Ms. Martinson's terrible ones

Yes! I totally agree we should tackle child poverty at KSJ tomorrow!

Hey, I thought you were going to wait for me after school on Friday?! It turns out Ian and I were the only ones who hadn't picked a topic by Thursday's deadline, so Ms. Martinson wanted to talk to us. First she suggested hieroglyphics, but Ian said if we researched ancient Egypt, we should turn ourselves into mummies and give our oral presentation while wrapped in bandages. I vetoed that idea. Then Ms. Martinson suggested illuminated manuscripts, which were apparently called "illuminated" because they had hand-drawn pictures and not because they were brilliant. I told Ms. Martinson (in my most diplomatic tone) that her suggestions were not applicable to modern life. Now we need to think of our own idea by Monday, or else.

By the way, did I see you and Drew leaving school together?

Dear Premier:

I am writing this letter on behalf of the Kids for Social Justice club, and also on behalf of hungry children. Compared to lots of places, our country is super-rich, but did you know that a third of the people using our food banks are kids? Please create better government policies so that kids don't go hungry.

Recently, my mom went to Myanmar (because my grandma got sick, and so: Big Family Emergency) and Dad was put in charge of cooking. Whoa! Now I have personally experienced what it's like to go to school hungry, or at least what it's like to go to school feeling gross because I ate two blueberry Toaster Strudels, which are not made of natural substances. No wonder some kids can't concentrate properly. And if they can't concentrate, they won't do well in school, and they won't graduate and get good jobs, and they won't pay taxes. Then you might run out of government money, Premier, all because you didn't give kids enough to eat.

So I hope you'll act quickly and promptly and immediately, and get those kids some real food. Bacon and eggs for the win!

(Or, if you're half-Asian like me, rice and eggs for the win!)

Sincerely,

Mya Parsons

Mya Parsons

Co-founder, Kids for Social Justice

MOM CALLED MONDAY NIGHT WHILE NANDA AND DAD were out picking up sushi. I got her all to myself and she had an amaZING suggestion for our communications project. After dinner, I used my whole half-hour of screen time on research, which proves exactly how dedicated I am to our new topic.

Thank goodness, because Ian and I had already missed the deadline for choosing an idea. Also, Ms. Martinson apparently told Mr. Gupta that I'm only allowed to schedule counseling sessions in the mornings, and not during our afternoon project time.

So much for doctor-patient confidentiality.

Ian and I dragged our desks directly under the windows, as far away from Cleo and Drew as possible. Not only because I wanted to keep my idea secret, but because Cleo and Drew were sitting on the same chair, Cleo sketching while Drew held the paper steady. Their heads were so close that one of them was probably inhaling what the other was exhaling. Oxygen deprivation explained a lot, actually.

Ian stared at them with his nose wrinkled.

"That's kind of —"

"Disgusting," I finished.

Then I looked at the floor for a while because it was a strange and uncomfortable experience to have agreed with Ian.

"I brought an idea," I said finally, pushing my papers toward him.

He read my first page of notes. "I thought we weren't allowed to do cell phones," he said.

I repeated my mom's brilliant suggestion. "Cell phones are only a *tool*. We're going to talk about texting, which is a communication *form* and just happens to use cell phones."

He gazed at the ceiling and seemed to be considering. I stared at the white pimple on his chin. Ian was obviously following the mom-advice that you're not supposed to pop pimples, but in my opinion that advice is a recipe for social disaster, and moms should restrict their advice to project ideas and not skincare.

Ian read my notes again. "We could do a fun slide show, all in texts," he said.

"And there's tons to talk about. We can include how texting developed, how emojis are approved, and the ways texting changes people's brains."

"It does?" Ian asked.

I was a little sketchy on that part. "We'll have to research it."

Ms. Martinson appeared above us, in that sudden and inconvenient way they learn in teacher's college.

"Texting," she said, sounding doubtful.

"It's different than cell phones," I said.

"Scientists think that texting might have neurological effects," Ian said.

I think Ms. Martinson and I were equally surprised that Ian could say "neurological." I could have hugged him if it weren't for the pimple issue.

"That's why this project is such a great opportunity," I said, in my best United Nations voice. "It will give us the chance to challenge ourselves."

"Why don't you sketch some ideas," Ms. Martinson said.

Then she disapparated, Harry Potter–style, which meant we'd won, which meant we were definitely for sure doing our project on texting, which was sort of like doing it on cell phones except even more amaZING.

By the end of our work time, Ian had drawn some comic book panels, and he went on (and on and on and on) to explain how we could use graphics and a slide show and a handout in our presentation.

He started divvying up our jobs.

"You won't need to write so much," I told him.

"You think it's going to be too long?" He looked concerned.

"It's not that. It's just that once I start writing, you don't need to be doing the same thing. We'll end up with doubles, and obviously, we'll be using the better version."

He seemed a little confused. Then he said, "That's actually something else I was thinking about."

I glazed over while he talked. I started thinking about Cleo's cell phone, and my lack thereof.

"Something . . . text bubbles . . . blah, blah, blah . . ."

Then Ian added three words with the potential to change my life.

"Multi-pronged strategy."

Multi. Pronged. Strategy.

"That's brilliant," I said.

His head popped up, his eyes widened, and his face turned red, so I didn't bother to explain that I hadn't been following his babbling, and I'd lost track of his plans after he began narrating his first cartoon strip with his first fake-Siri voice. Instead, I was thinking of how I could transfer his approach—his "multi-pronged strategy"—to my cell-phone issues.

It was exactly the plan I needed.

To: cleocleobear@gmail.com
From: myamyapapaya1@gmail.com
Subject: Color advice

I got your message but it was too late to call you back. Sorry I wasn't there for you in your time of project need. If it's not too late, I think you should use the turquoise paper for the main display and the yellow as the accent color. It will be super gorgeous!

Also, I've got the perfect way to convince my parents that I need a cell phone. A multi-pronged strategy. Call me. ASAP!!!

NINE HOURS OF SLEEP A NIGHT. THAT'S HOW MUCH TEN-to seventeen-year-olds need in order to develop properly and be able to create multi-pronged strategies. I looked it up. Plus, Mom was right. Kids who get more sleep have higher IQs.

All of this meant my sister was basically ruining (a) my chances of getting a cell phone, (b) my future university career and (c) my life in general.

Twice in the past week, she'd had nightmares and woken me up. This time, she sat bolt upright in bed and said, "The water."

"The what?" I asked, because I didn't realize she was sleep-talking.

"What are we going to do about the water?"

"Do you want me to get you some?" If it meant I could go back to sleep, I would do pretty much anything, even walk to the bathroom and pour water that Nanda was perfectly capable of pouring for herself.

"NO!" she said. "Don't go in there! It's too deep." She looked around with a terrified expression on her face, as if her bed were floating in an alligator-infested river.

I finally caught on.

"Nanda, there's no water."

This didn't help. She started to wheeze, and cry, and call for Mom, and babble things about water that made NO

SENSE, until I finally said, "Nanda, if you go back to sleep, I'll get rid of the water. I promise it will be gone by morning."

She flopped back onto her pillow. About five seconds later, she started to snore.

Dad was also snoring. I could hear him, all the way down the hall. Which was hardly appropriate parenting, and not good for my brain development either.

I lay in bed for a while, listening to my IQ points slowly drain away.

I STARTED WORK ON MY MULTI-PRONGED STRATEGY ON Thursday afternoon. I was brainstorming at the kitchen table when Dad walked in. I hurriedly flipped over my paper. I hadn't heard him arrive home, and I definitely wasn't ready to reveal my plan.

He sank into the chair across from me, let his head flop back and closed his eyes. His hair was wet from the rain. He looked pale.

"You probably have low blood sugar. We should eat something," I told him. "What are we having for dinner?"

He made a noise somewhere between a groan and a grunt.

"Do you know what Ms. Martinson told us today in our health class? Tweens and teens who don't have dinner with their families are four times more likely to drink and do drugs and get cyberbullied."

Groan-grunt.

"But we should hurry, because Nanda has soccer in an hour."

This time, it was definitely a groan.

We ate ramen noodles, then Dad and Nanda rushed out the door. I watched a whole episode of *Dancing with the Stars* while they were gone AND I worked on my strategy. Dad's main arguments had been (a) a cell phone is expensive, (b) I might lose it or use it inappropriately and (c) satellite signals could scramble my brain. I wasn't sure he was serious about that last one, but I included it just in case. And I had almost perfected my plans. Almost.

High Cost	⟶ Pay 50%	⟶ babysitting
		⟶ dog walking? (small dogs!)
Responsibility	⟶ Prove	⟶ pick up Nanda after school
		⟶ continue excellent grades
		⟶ look into Cleo's no-boob-texting seminar
		⟶ more????
Brain damage	⟶ Research	⟶ print studies and statistics
		⟶ copy Cleo's report card
	⟶ Recruit	⟶ talk to Cleo's mom
		⟶ get Auntie Winnie on board

I was still trying to decide whether babysitting, dog walking and picking up Nanda after school would serve as money-making schemes AND be enough to prove I was a reliable person. Did I need to create a fake cell phone and carry it around for a week, to show I wouldn't lose it? If anyone saw it at school, I'd look like an idiot, pretending a piece of cardboard was my new phone.

Before I came to any conclusions, Nanda and Dad arrived home, looking as though they'd rolled around in mud for an hour and a half.

"Change your clothes, then come right back," Dad told Nanda. "We're having a family meeting."

Nanda peeled off her jacket and threw it on top of her cleats, socks and shin pads before racing up the stairs.

Dad looked at the pile and made his new noise again.

"Bad practice?" I asked.

"We'll talk about it at our meeting," he said. Then he picked up Nanda's stuff and *crackle-crackle-crackled* his way up the stairs.

I went to the kitchen and put a package of popcorn in the microwave, because a proper meeting should have snacks, and that's the kind of responsible, reliable planner I was.

Once we were all sitting in the living room, and Nanda was stuffing her face with popcorn as if she'd never seen food before, Dad cleared his throat.

"You're making a lot of weird sounds today," I said. "I think it's a guy thing. At lunchtime, Drew and Ian decided to burp everything they said."

Dad actually chuckled. "I used to do that."

My sister proceeded to burp: "Whaaat iiiiis ooooour meeeeeeting abooooout?" I had to look away so I wouldn't see the bits of half-chewed popcorn in her mouth.

"About chooooores," Dad burped back.

"You're both disgusting." Our meeting had gone completely off the rails, all because I happened to mention something that happened in class. The experts might have been wrong about the benefits of family time.

"Did you say 'chores'?" Nanda wrinkled her nose. Then she peeled off one of her socks and bent low over her foot. "One of my toes is hurting."

"I heard from your mom," Dad said, crossing his arms and looking much more serious. "Grandma's getting better, but not as quickly as they'd hoped."

"What does that mean?" I asked.

"They think she has a secondary infection. She's going to take another round of antibiotics. If they work, Mom will be ready to come home. But best-case scenario . . . another week."

"Another week! It's already been six billion weeks."

"Four and a half, actually," Dad said.

"I think my toe is infected," Nanda said.

"Worst-case scenario?" I asked.

"Amputation," she said, but Dad and I ignored her.

"They're both doing the best they can," he said.

A little dagger of Mom-missing stabbed me between the ribs, and suddenly it felt as if the world might fall apart if she stayed away any longer.

"I can't keep eating burnt broccoli and Toaster Strudels, and wearing dirty clothes, *and* looking after Nanda after school forever," I protested.

"Well, I can't keep cooking *caramelized* broccoli and washing your clothes and looking after both of you by myself," Dad said, in a voice that made him sound even more like Drew or Ian than he did when he was burping his words. "I'm in court next week."

Ugh. Whenever one of Dad's cases went to court, he spent all his evenings buried in papers, with a canyon-deep furrow between his eyebrows.

"Is this when you sell us on Craigslist?" I asked. "Two orphans, ten bucks or best offer?"

Nanda sniffed, and both Dad and I swiveled to stare at her just as her nose dripped into the popcorn bowl.

"Nanda! Gross! And I wasn't serious."

Dad pulled her onto his lap and started murmuring to her as if she were a baby.

Sighing, I got up to look at her toe. Sure enough, the little dude in the middle was red and filled with pus along one side. "You have an ingrown nail."

"I know!" she said. "But only Mom can fix them!"

And that's when I had my epiphany. (Word courtesy of Ms. Martinson's spelling test.)

Here's what I realized: family members are a lot like toe-nails. Most of the time, you can assume they're functioning properly. They're there, doing what they're supposed to do. But every once in a while, there's a crisis, and you can't take them for granted anymore.

Watching my sister snivel to Dad on the couch, I knew I was seeing an ingrown nail bigger than the one on Nanda's foot. Our family was falling apart. If we didn't get a grip on this whole food/clothing/schedule thing, we were going to end up in a big mess of pus.

Unfortunately, before I could come up with one of my new specialty multi-pronged strategies, one that could address our situation, Dad announced that *he'd* made a plan. Then he shifted Nanda to the floor and took notes out of his pocket. NOTES!

"Groceries, I'll take care of," he said.

"I'll make you a list," I said quickly. Broccoli would *not* be on it, or bananas either.

"Nanda, you're officially in charge of laundry," he continued. "You can start one load before school every day, and one load after school. If you put the dry clothes on the couch, we'll all help fold them."

"Do I get paid?" Nanda asked.

"No," he said. Then, ignoring her whine, he leveled his gaze at me. "Mya, I'm going to need you to be completely reliable about picking up Nanda. You can take her to skateboarding on Wednesdays and help her get ready for soccer on Thursdays."

"Okay . . ." I said. If this was my only job, I was going to do a secret happy dance as soon as I left the room.

He squashed that dream like a piece of popcorn into the carpet.

"And I'll call Auntie Winnie. She said she'd give you some cooking lessons. You can start after school one day next week."

Hearing those words was exactly as horrifying as squeezing the goo from an ingrown nail. Exactly.

"I can't—" I started.

"You can't do all the cooking, obviously. But you and Auntie Winnie can practice a few dishes, and we'll happily eat the results."

"I'm not—"

"Mya, we all need to pitch in."

"But what if I wanted to pitch in in a different way? Scrub toilets? Or clean chimneys?"

"Scrubbing toilets is not a bad idea. You can tackle the bathrooms while we get a day organized with Winnie."

"What!? That's—"

"Nanda, you can sweep the entrance hall and pick up your soccer clothes and tidy the shoes," he said, before I could even say, "a massive injustice."

After that, Dad slapped his palms together, as if he'd just solved the problems of the world, and sent Nanda and me to get ready for bed.

"And you're fine," he told Nanda. "Your toe will be better in a day or two."

This didn't seem to help.

"Ow. Ow. Ow," she said with every step.

"Stop whining," I told her.

"But it hurts!"

"I'll cut your nail properly, and you can soak it in the bathtub."

"You know how?" She looked up at me as if I were secretly a surgeon. It was a nice look, and it temporarily distracted me from the horror that was Dad's chores list.

"Let's beep-sume that I can handle one toe."

Even though I had excellent personal hygiene, it was possible that I might have conceivably—once—had an ingrown toenail of my own. I knew exactly what Mom had done.

I cut a tiny triangle in the top of Nanda's toenail so it would grow straight again, then I promised to put cream on it and bandage it after her bath. She was so grateful that I even poured her water and added Epsom salts.

After that, I lay on my bed thinking about all the cooking torture in store for me. I could only find one silver lining: Cleo and I wouldn't have to search for a KSJ topic for a while. There would be plenty of child labor going on right in my very own house.

To: cleocleobear@gmail.com
From: myamyapapaya1@gmail.com
Subject: Stupendous idea

Thanks for planning tomorrow's KSJ meeting! I had some ideas, of course, but I'm willing to save them for future weeks. We should definitely tackle the Iran situation first.

How did you hear about this case? I can't believe Iran would throw that woman in jail just for writing a story about not stoning people. Um . . . hello? Obviously they shouldn't kill people by throwing stones at them. That is SO twentieth century. And I read the link you sent. She hadn't even published the story! The police found it on her laptop.

You'll have to figure out how to pronounce Golrokh
Ebrahimi Iraee before the meeting. Good luck with that!

To: p.lwyn@hotmail.com
From: myamyapapaya1@gmail.com
Subject: Everything under control

Dear Mom,
We are missing you like crazy, especially since Nanda accidentally
put one of Dad's highlighters in the wash with his work pants and
my favorite sweater and RUINED them completely.

Dad says that you have to stay with Grandma a little bit
longer. Don't worry about us while you're away. I've seized the
reins. Taken charge. I'm captaining the ship. By the time you
come home, things will be running so smoothly around here
that you'll wonder if you're even needed. Though of course
you are, and you'll want to jump right back into family life, so
we'll be okay handing over some of our new responsibilities,
including bathroom cleaning. But don't worry one bit until
then. I've got things covered.

By the way, do you think I should put some offerings on the
shrine while you're gone? We wouldn't want Buddha starving
to death, right? I would have done this earlier, but Toaster
Strudels seemed sacrilegious.

I found the manual for our rice cooker in the junk drawer
and I actually made rice yesterday. Pretty impressive, don't
you think? Now we can have hot rice for breakfast instead

of Toaster Strudels, and I'm pretty sure Buddha will like that better, the way all normal people do except Nanda.

Do you (a) say prayers when you put the food there or (b) just leave the offering? If the answer is (a), are you allowed to pray for anything you want? Just wondering.

Love,
Mya

PS In case you and Grandma are staying away because Dad's hair is SO embarrassing, you'll be happy to hear that he got it cut. At the barbershop. For twelve dollars. It's not exactly high fashion, but it's probably acceptable enough that you can risk re-entering the country.

PART III

FIVE WEEKS WITHOUT MOM

THERE WAS A NEW SIXTH GRADER AT OUR KSJ meeting yesterday, named Emilia.

While Cleo and I talked to everyone about writers getting imprisoned in Iran, Emilia stared at us with her mouth hanging open. Then, when it was time to write, she finished TWO letters.

"Are you going to come back?" I asked her at the end. "We meet every week."

"I have to ask my mom if we can afford it," she said.

"It's free."

"It's FREE?"

Drew snorted, but Cleo hit him, so that was good.

"You can bring friends," I suggested.

"I CAN?"

It was the best moment of my day. Sometimes, changing the world is awesome.

WHEN I GOT TO SCHOOL ON TUESDAY MORNING, CLEO was sitting on top of a desk in the hallway, with her earbuds in and her legs swinging. She was wearing a pink T-shirt and I realized for the first time that Cleo had boobs. Not big boobs, but still . . . something.

I'd almost reached her when JoJo bounced up and flicked the bud from Cleo's ear.

"I got your text. Do you think it will happen today?" JoJo asked.

Cleo shrugged, a giant grin on her face. "Maybe."

JoJo grabbed her hands and they both squealed.

"Today what?" I asked as I joined them.

JoJo pressed her lips together as if she had a major secret. Something only people with boobs could know, apparently.

I used to like JoJo. At the beginning of sixth grade, we did a project together about water pollution. We painted wooden fish and wired them to the fences above the playground drains to remind everyone that chemicals running down storm drains go right to the ocean. We got an A+ on the project and Principal Richards wrote a special note on the bottom of our report cards that term to tell our parents how hard we'd worked.

This year, we hadn't been hanging out as often. She'd got her period over the summer (which she told us about IN DETAIL on the first day of school), and she'd had a boyfriend at summer camp (which she also told us about IN DETAIL) and she seemed . . . different.

When the warning bell rang, I turned toward the classroom. But Cleo grabbed my arm and pulled me close.

"I think Drew is going to kiss me," she whispered in my ear.

"Eww," I said automatically, which sent them both into hysterical laughter. Cleo practically fell off her table.

Once I realized that Cleo actually *wanted* Drew to kiss her, I tried to think of something more positive to say, but the second bell rang and our homeroom teacher waved us all inside.

Then, during Mr. Kapoor's math class, I couldn't stop staring at Drew's nose. It's a large nose. A specimen of nose-dom. And Cleo's nose is normal, but not exactly button-sized. How were they going to kiss without their noses bumping?

Of course I've seen tons of people kiss before. Couples in movies. Even my parents, in my own kitchen, though Nanda and I try to discourage that sort of behavior. But suddenly, I couldn't figure out the mechanics. People must need to tilt their heads in different directions. What if one person leans in and tilts his head in one direction and the other person leans in and tilts her head in the same direction at the same time? How do people negotiate the angle of nose-tilt in advance, so they don't bump? It seemed very complicated.

"Mya, is there something wrong with your neck?" Mr. Kapoor asked, and I realized I was staring at Drew with my head cricked to one side.

"No." I'm sure I flushed bright red, but no one seemed to notice.

At lunchtime, I cornered Cleo before she could sit down beside Drew and start living her romantic fantasies. I dragged her into the girls' bathroom and checked under the stall doors to make sure there were no other visitors.

"How come JoJo knew about the kissing thing before I did?" I asked.

Cleo unclipped her purse (since when does Cleo carry a purse?), took out a baggie of supplies and started brushing her teeth. Before lunch. As if Drew was going to leap out at any moment and plant a big one on her lips. I stared at Cleo in the mirror, wondering if it were possible that my friend had been abducted by aliens and replaced by a tooth-brushing, breast-growing, JoJo-texting impostor.

"Well, I fifn't want to falk abouf if ouf loud," she said. Then she spit. "What if my mom heard me? But I think it almost happened yesterday. I was so excited, I had to tell someone."

"You couldn't email me?"

"Emails aren't private! What if your dad saw the screen?" she said.

"What if JoJo's mom saw your text?"

"I don't even know JoJo's mom."

There had to be a flaw in that logic somewhere. But more importantly: "What do you mean, it *almost* happened?"

At that moment, a group of sixth-grade girls poured into the bathroom, shrieking because one of them had bubble-gum in her hair. They were about to try to brush it out when I stopped them. If any of them had a sister like mine, they'd have known how to handle this sort of crisis. "You need peanut butter or vegetable oil," I told them.

"No one has peanut butter at school!" the girl with the gum-hair squealed.

"Go to the lunchroom and check the cupboard the cooking classes use. They'll have vegetable oil."

She looked at me as if I were an angel specifically assigned to the girls' bathroom.

Crisis management was going to be my thing one day. Not to brag, but in that sort of situation, I tend to be amaZING.

Unfortunately, by the time I'd herded them all out of the bathroom, Cleo had finished her brushing. I had to hurry after her out the door and toward the cafeteria. Then, when I sat down with my tray, she was tossing raisins into the air, and Drew was trying to catch them with his mouth. At that moment, his mouth looked even less attractive than usual. It definitely wasn't something I would ever want to kiss, even if the nose issue were solved.

Speaking of the nose issue, I'd read in books about people practicing by kissing their pillows. That night, after Nanda finished with her snot wiping and began to snore, and before I turned on my secret-journal-writing flashlight, I tried it out. It was unhelpful. For one thing, my pillow had no nose. Also, everything was mushy.

Maybe people in books had firmer pillows than I did.

AUNTIE WINNIE COULDN'T DO OUR FIRST COOKING lesson until the weekend, and I couldn't eat one more meal of rice and scrambled egg. I was sure I had scurvy from vitamin deficiencies. Or rickets. Or leprosy.

Dad didn't get home until almost seven o'clock on Wednesday night because of his big case. By that time, Nanda and I had eaten two bowls of cereal and one blueberry Toaster Strudel each, and I was feeling a little nauseated. I was even more nauseated when I saw the scrambled eggs.

"Again?"

"What are you talking about?" Dad said. "I ate this every single night of law school, and I loved it."

Then he put a big scoop of eggs on my plate but they weren't cooked enough and I almost threw up.

"They look like baby chicken brains!"

Nanda decided not to eat hers either.

"What do you want, then?" Dad said, pressing his fingers to his forehead. I could tell the carbs were really getting to him.

"Pizza," Nanda said.

"I don't have pizza."

"Another strudel," Nanda said.

So he made her one, which Mom would never, ever have done. I was beginning to see why Mom didn't buy those things.

He asked what I wanted, but by that time I really wasn't feeling well and I went to bed.

Not for long, though. Lying there, I remembered I was supposed to have a multi-pronged strategy to get my cell phone. I needed to concentrate on the other prongs.

BABYSITTING!

REASONABLY PRICED! RELIABLE!

Hi! I'm Mya! I have my Red Cross babysitting certification and I'd love to watch your children for you while you shop, work or enjoy a (well-deserved!) date night.

Please don't hesitate to contact me at the number below. It's my home number as, unfortunately, I do not have my own cell phone.

Looking forward to hearing from you!!
604-555-7830

604-555-7830
604-555-7830
604-555-7830
604-555-7830
604-555-7830
604-555-7830
604-555-7830
604-555-7830
604-555-7830

Dear Mrs. Sanders,

I've made a poster to advertise my new babysitting services, and I'm going to pop one into your mailbox with this note.

It was nice to see you at the elementary school today with your little boys. Those two are so cute! My mom always says she can tell that they're brothers because they have the same number of freckles.

I noticed that when one was throwing gravel at the other in the playground, you seemed a bit tired. My mom says motherhood is the toughest job on Earth, so I guess I can understand.

Call me anytime you need a break!

Your one-block-away neighbor,

Mya Parsons

Mya Parsons

I GOT 14/15 ON OUR FRACTIONS TEXT. WHICH WOULD HAVE been amaZING except that Cleo and Drew both got 15/15.

They were all, "Twinsies!"

Ms. Martinson rearranged our desks into rows of three. Ian was evicted to the row behind us, but I still had Drew on one side of me and Cleo on the other. When Drew wanted to say something to Cleo—for example, "Hey, great minds think alike"—he leaned over my desk and sprinkled me with all his germs and stray skin cells.

And what a dumb thing to say. "Great minds think alike." Even more dumb was the WAY Drew said it, with a side serving of eyebrow-wiggle. I threw up a little in my mouth.

Fortunately, Ms. Martinson distracted me by announcing project work.

"It's the middle of October," she said. "You should be making significant progress."

That was fine, because I was mentally prepared. Twenty-four hours earlier, I'd been *freaking out*. I'd found one scientific article about the effects of texting on the brain, and it said a whole bunch of terrible stuff about texts basically ruining kids' attention span. So obviously we couldn't use that. Then I'd found another study about brain waves and it made NO SENSE.

I couldn't understand any of it. But I emailed my mom in the midst of my confusion and . . . drum roll, please . . . it turns out Mom has superior science-reading skills, which probably explains the whole career-in-editing thing. Her email said, "I understand the basic points, which are all anyone understands."

Thanks to her, I had a couple pages of notes and several typed-out quotes, all ready for me and Ian to use in our project.

"I've figured things out for us," I said, once we'd arranged our stuff outside the class. Some groups were working at their desks, and some in the library, but Ian and I claimed one side of the hallway, and Cleo and Drew claimed the other.

"When they're texting, people have to use language AND

coordinate their hands and fingers, obviously, AND figure out the emotions behind the words."

"Most people text with their thumbs."

I chose to ignore his interruption, because: high road. "Texting causes a whole new kind of brain activity."

"It also changes how we think about things," Ian said. "People used to write long letters to each other and share their big, deep thoughts, but now they write quick texts about what they had for lunch."

"I don't think we should jump to conclusions," I said.

"We should talk about texting while driving, too. And texting while walking."

"Absolutely not."

Ian crossed his arms, obviously waiting for further enlightenment.

"There's enough prejudice against texting in the world. We need to be careful not to stereotype."

Ian pushed one of his cartoons toward me. It showed a walking-texting guy completely blocking a sidewalk, with strollers and dogs and joggers all piled up behind him.

"Okay, this is pretty funny," I admitted. And at least he wasn't armpit farting while I talked.

Then I reached my big finale: "We need to focus on the fact that texting creates unique brain waves, so people are practically evolving every time they send a message."

Ian didn't look as impressed as I expected. But I was impressed with myself. And seriously, thank God for the Internet, which was probably also changing my brain, because it had allowed Mom to help me with this project all the way from Myanmar. Plus, she sent me links that actually made sense and now I was totally ready to **WOW!** Ms. Martinson.

"Are we still going to do comic strips and a slide show and handouts? With text bubbles?" Ian asked.

"Good thinking. That's exactly what I was going to suggest. Pretty soon, you won't need my input at all," I said.

He would always need my suggestions, of course, but I wanted to sound encouraging.

To: p.lwyn@hotmail.com
From: myamyapapaya1@gmail.com
Subject: Current events

Please give six billion kisses to Grandma from all of us here, even though Dad and Nanda are at soccer, so I'm the only one thinking about you at this exact moment.

Dad said Grandma's new antibiotics seem to be helping—YAY and DOUBLE YAY!

But I can't believe the Rohingya situation is getting worse. Making progress in this world is seriously difficult. Did you know that writers are still getting imprisoned in Iran too? AND there are ridiculous levels of child poverty pretty much everywhere? I'm going to have to fast-track myself to the United Nations so we can get things done.

Speaking of the United Nations, they have their regional headquarters in Geneva, Switzerland, and you know what that means. I'm going to be eating fondue every single day! I hope you're not too old to come visit me, because then we can agree that double-dipping is allowed.

Crossing my fingers to see you SOON and DOUBLE SOON!

I WAS SO HAPPY WHEN THE FINAL BELL RANG ON FRIDAY and it was officially the weekend. My brain was FRIED from trying to work on a communications project with someone who communicates mainly in burps.

I threw on my jacket and went in search of Nanda. But I only got to the border between the schoolyards, where the bamboo grows against the fence and all the little kids play hide-and-seek at lunch hour. Because who was standing there? Cleo and Drew. They'd somehow beaten me out of the school and planted themselves amidst the branches, leaning against the chain-link.

And just as I walked up, he KISSED HER NOSE. A little peck on the tip of it.

Then Cleo kissed his nose.

THEN SHE KISSED HIM FOR REAL.

ON THE LIPS.

The whole time, I stood there like an idiot with my mouth hanging open. Fortunately, I pulled myself together before they noticed me and I backed away, then sped across the playground toward the elementary school.

I found Nanda on her way down the main stairs, holding her skateboard.

"Are you okay?" she asked. "You look blotchy."

"I'm fine," I said. But I didn't talk to her the whole way to the skateboard park. Once we got there, I sat on a concrete curb at the edge of the ramps and squeezed my head between my hands.

"Mya, watch this!" Nanda called.

I plastered a smile on my face and pretended to watch. What I was really seeing was a replay of something that happened last year.

A group of students from Sweden had visited our school for the day, and Cleo and I were chosen to show one of them around. At lunchtime, as Cleo and I were joking with each other, the student said, "I can tell you two are knowing each other very well."

I nodded, smiling. "We finish each other's—"

Cleo grabbed my ham and cheese right out of my hand and said, "Sandwiches!"

Then, with her mouth full of my lunch, she told the student, "That's an English phrase. When you know each other really well, you say you finish each other's sandwiches."

Sitting on the curb in the skateboard park, I had this horrible feeling that Cleo and Drew were finishing each other's sandwiches, and Cleo didn't really care what was in my lunch anymore.

In the middle of my worrying, one of Nanda's little buddies bailed off his board at the top of the ramp and slid backward down the concrete. His dad ran across to pick him up, but he was already wailing. There was a giant road-rash scrape across his cheek and his chin.

I knew exactly how he felt.

DAD LUGGED HOME A HUGE BOX OF FILES AND SPREAD them across the dining room table. He spent most of Saturday morning pretending our house was his office, which meant Nanda and I had to tiptoe around like ninjas. When we tried to turn on the TV, he gave us a lecture on the dangers of procrastination and the importance of getting math homework done, even though (a) Nanda didn't have any homework, (b) Mom always says it's our own responsibility to schedule our studying and (c) every other child in North America spends Saturday mornings watching TV.

By the time I finished my math, Nanda was using my bed as a parachute landing pad for army men (SO seriously abnormal). I went downstairs, where Dad was sitting in front of his papers with his hands folded and his eyes closed.

I listened for snores. Nothing.

"What are you doing?"

His head popped up.

"Saying a prayer." He looked a little embarrassed.

Even though Mom was a Buddhist and Dad a Christian, we didn't usually go to temple or to church. Just for weddings and funerals. Or sometimes to the Alliance church down the street at Easter, or the temple when there was a food festival. (At the food festivals, there were tons and tons of different curries and baked rice dishes and deep-fried samosas, all really cheap, so we would become dedicated Buddhists for the day.)

But this was beside the point.

"What are you praying about?" I asked Dad.

"About your mom getting home safe and the house not burning down while she's gone."

Which was a reasonable fear, if Nanda one day decided she needed explosions to go with her army men.

"Mom keeps an extinguisher under the sink, and they teach us at school how to crawl out of the house if there's a fire."

"Well, that's one thing off my list of worries," Dad said.

But he didn't look as relieved as I expected.

AUNTIE WINNIE DEFINITELY CAME PREPARED. ON SUNDAY morning, my skateboarding sister had to pause her driveway tricks to carry a box of ingredients inside. Auntie Winnie bustled through the front door after her and handed me a binder as if she were presenting a treasure chest.

The binder was filled with recipes that she'd typed and printed for me. There must have been twenty or thirty, at least.

"Mom's supposed to be back any day!"

"There's no reason you can't keep helping after your mother gets home. It's ridiculous that she does all the cooking around here," Auntie Winnie said.

Nanda ducked back outside. She was smarter than she looked.

"Dad does the dishes," I said weakly.

"And what do you do?" Auntie Winnie raised her eyebrows.

I opened my mouth to protest, because I'd been doing a LOT around the house (including rewashing the laundry load that Nanda left sitting in the machine for two days, growing mildew). But I was pretty sure Auntie Winnie was asking what I did to help when Mom *was* around, and I couldn't think of anything. I was an incredibly helpful person. I just couldn't think of anything at that moment.

"The base of all these curries is a mix of onions, ginger, garlic . . ." Rattling off ingredients, she washed her hands quickly and pulled out Mom's food processor. For a few minutes, I thought maybe she'd cook the entire curry, and I could nod at appropriate intervals.

Or not.

"Get your hands washed," she said.

Before you could say "upcoming catastrophe," I was smashing garlic cloves with the back of a giant knife, peeling off the papery parts, and putting the rest into the food processor. After that, in went an onion, peeled ginger, turmeric, paprika and cayenne. I almost mixed up the amounts on the paprika and cayenne, but Auntie Winnie caught me in time. She looked at me as if I had some sort of learning disability. Which I did: culinary dyslexia.

It's a thing.

They just haven't discovered it yet.

Auntie Winnie heated some oil in a big pot, then told me to scrape the paste from the food processor. And that was when the catastrophe part happened.

I guess I was supposed to use a spoon or something. I reached in with my hand. I thought I was being careful, but as I scooped out the paste, I nicked my finger on the edge of the food processor blade.

I squealed.

Auntie Winnie squealed. She was louder.

It was hard to tell if I was bleeding or if it was curry paste. But at that moment, Nanda appeared at the kitchen door, still in her skateboarding gear, with blood streaming from her nose. It was definitely not curry paste, and there was enough of it to spatter the front of her shirt. She looked like something from a horror movie.

"I need some beep-sistance," she said.

Auntie Winnie turned from brown to white, and then a little bit green. I'd always thought "turned green" was an imaginary thing, but apparently it was real.

She reached behind her, flapping her hand until she caught hold of the table edge, then she sank into a kitchen chair.

Nanda and I stared at each other over her head.

"Something's burning," said Nanda, which made an air bubble appear in her nose blood.

I turned off the stove with my non-bloody hand, which I thought showed good ability to think in a crisis.

"Are you okay?" Nanda and I asked Auntie Winnie at the same time.

She had her head between her knees. "Do we need to call an ambulance?" she asked from down there.

"For us or for you?" Nanda said.

"You!"

Nanda glanced at me. Her nose was still in the right place, so I shook my head and passed her a dish towel for the blood. I wrapped another one around my finger.

"No ambulance," Nanda said.

"I guess you don't like blood?" I asked my auntie.

She groaned. "I'm not good with nursing. We're lucky it's your mom and not me looking after your grandma right now."

I loved Auntie Winnie, of course, because she was my aunt and you had to love your aunts, but seeing her with her head between her legs was the first time I actually liked her. It was as if, at that moment, she turned into a real person.

Though not an entirely helpful person.

"C'mon," I told Nanda. "The laundry's still on the couch. We'll find you a new shirt. Don't take the towel away from your nose for a few more minutes."

By the time I got back to the kitchen, Auntie Winnie was a normal color again. She'd scraped our burnt onions from the pot and started again. She chopped the chicken and tomatoes herself, but I added them. And I measured the fish sauce and sprinkled in the cilantro. At the end of it all, Auntie Winnie said there was hope for me yet.

Then Nanda showed up and asked her if she knew any good tips for getting blood out of a beige dish towel. Auntie Winnie said to throw it in the garbage. She'd buy a new one, and Mom would never know.

"Auntie Winnie, I think there's hope for you yet," I said.

THIEVES' CHICKEN

(Auntie Winnie says it's called Thieves' Chicken because if you steal a chicken, this is the fastest way to cook it. She bought hers at the grocery store, though, which is lucky. I would NOT have wanted to see it with the feathers attached.)

1 onion
3 cloves garlic
Peeled thumb-sized piece of fresh ginger
1 teaspoon turmeric
1 tablespoon paprika
½ teaspoon cayenne pepper
¼ cup vegetable oil
2 diced tomatoes
3 tablespoons fish sauce
2 cups water
2 stalks lemongrass, peeled and crushed
10 bone-in chicken thighs

Put onion, garlic and ginger in a food processor and blend until smooth. Or grate them, but don't grate your fingers. Add spices and stir. In a large pot, heat oil to medium. Add curry paste and cook, stirring often, for 4 to 5 minutes, adding water if the mixture begins to stick. Add tomatoes and fish sauce and cook another 5 minutes. Add water, lemongrass stalks and chicken, and bring to a boil. Reduce heat and simmer for about 45 minutes, until chicken is tender.

To: p.lwyn@hotmail.com
From: myamyapapaya1@gmail.com
Subject: Your daughter, chef extraordinaire

Hi Mom!

It was nice to talk to you tonight, but your calls never seem long enough. Dad and Nanda hog the phone. I'm going to tell Dad that he's an adult, and therefore capable of independence. He should get a smaller share of your time.

Anyway, I'm glad Grandma's slowly feeling better, and you shouldn't worry about us here. Not one bit. Things were crazy after you left, but now I've taken charge and everything's running smoothly. Nanda's learned to do laundry. You may need a new white sweater, because I borrowed yours (sorry), and then Nanda washed it (she should be double sorry). But isn't one white sweater a small price to pay to have your family wearing clean clothes? Exactly.

Miss you and love you tons,
Your fashionable daughter,
Mya
xoxoxoxoxo

WE WENT TO THE "IMAGINE HALLOWEEN" POP-UP store Thursday evening on the way to Nanda's soccer practice. We'd finally faced the fact that Mom wasn't going to be home in time to sew Nanda a magician's cape or to help me design a Mother Teresa costume.

After Dad vetoed several zombie masks and one really skimpy magician's assistant outfit (with tassels), Nanda decided to be a beep-stronaut. I chose a crazy 1970s disco outfit because (a) it had giant peace-sign earrings, which I was determined to work into every one of my outfits, forever, and (b) Dad said if I didn't choose something soon, he was going to come to my school dressed as a mermaid.

He would have too.

To: cleocleobear@gmail.com
From: myamyapapaya1@gmail.com
Subject: Changing the world

Thanks for the sketches of your new clothing line!! I LOVE the sunglasses frames that look like candy. You could totally donate part of your profits to refugee relief too, and then you'll be famous AND you'll be saving people.

I checked the UN website today. Their refugee agency is trying to get food and water to HALF A MILLION (!!!) Rohingya people who've now crossed the border from Myanmar to Bangladesh. It looks completely crazy-pants.

Also, the UN refugee agency has literally thousands of people working for it. They're going to need a reliable employee such as myself to keep them all organized. And I'll wear your ultra-fashionable clothes to work every day!

PS You're going to tell *me* your costume, right?

Mrs. Sanders, who I was supposed to call Cheryl, called me on Saturday.

"Hello, is Mya there?" she said, in an ultra professional voice.

"This is Mya," I said.

I thought that was ultra professional of me too! I was seriously *destined* for this occupation.

"Are you available next ----- night?"

I didn't hear which night because there was some sort of World War III in the background. Then Mrs. Sanders started yelling, which almost broke my eardrums. I had to hold the phone away from my ear until she switched back to her professional voice.

"Next Friday night?" she repeated.

Then she said, "IF I HEAR ANOTHER WORD, I AM THROWING YOU OUT THE WINDOW!" but I was quite sure she wasn't referring to me.

Fortunately, her yelling gave me time to frantically motion to Dad and make sure I was free on Friday.

"Yes, I would love to babysit."

She sounded VERY happy.

And with that, I embarked on my life as an income-earner. My cell phone was one step closer to existence!

PART IV

SEVEN WEEKS WITHOUT MOM

S OMETIMES, AS A UNITED NATIONS EMPLOYEE, YOU have to know when to take a break. For example, the UN negotiator left the peace talks in Syria when he didn't feel the two sides were trying hard enough.

I needed a serious mental break after KSJ on Monday. We were supposed to write letters to a journalist who was imprisoned in Egypt and sentenced to seven years, but then released at the last minute to return to Canada and teach university students about freedom of the press.

That's what we were SUPPOSED to do.

What we did do? Talk about costumes.

Things weren't too bad until someone asked Cleo what she was going to wear to school for Halloween. She refused to tell, and the rest of the meeting was entirely taken up by people guessing.

Cleo is apparently not dressing as a cat, a witch, Hermione Granger, a scarecrow, Princess Leia, a ballet dancer, a zombie ballet dancer, a bride, a zombie bride, a skeleton, a unicorn, a dragon, a pirate or a zombie pirate.

We'd have to save the world extra well next week.

AUNTIE WINNIE CAME OVER ON TUESDAY NIGHT TO hand out candy while I took Nanda trick-or-treating.

Personally, I think trick-or-treating is a parental obligation and not one that should be skipped in favor of work. But when I told this to Auntie Winnie, she sighed and took both my hands in hers.

"Your dad is juggling so much these days," she said. "We all have to pull together until your mom gets home. I know you must be feeling a bit sad and missing them both."

Which was ridiculous because I was practically a teenager and did not need constant supervision. Nanda, on the other hand, had her mouth stuffed full of chocolate and we hadn't even left the house yet.

"Let's go," I told her.

She squealed and jumped up and down in some sort of candy-induced fit.

"Aren't you dressing up, Mya?" Auntie Winnie asked.

"I'm too old," I said, because I didn't feel like explaining that (a) I wasn't in a disco mood and (b) the humongous peace signs had turned my earlobes green.

I was probably the only seventh grader in the entire world going house to house, and I wanted it absolutely clear that I was supervising and NOT trick-or-treating.

Cleo and Drew and JoJo and Rahul were all going to the theater to see *Razor*.

Even though my dad's parenting might not have been perfectly on point, he was still doing a better job than Cleo's mom. That movie was seriously inappropriate. I would never have gone, even if they had invited me.

To: cleocleobear@gmail.com
From: myamyapapaya1@gmail.com
Subject: Happy Halloween

You probably tried to call me before the movie, but I was busy, busy, busy!

I LOVED the Jane Goodall and chimpanzee costumes you and Drew wore to school. That was SUCH a good idea! Almost as good as two years ago when you and I went as matching coffee cups and put information on our backs about recycling.

You might have thought I was upset this morning when I excused myself to go to the bathroom, but I really had to pee. It totally makes sense that you asked Drew to be your costume partner instead of me this year, because obviously I wouldn't have wanted to wear a chimpanzee costume, and it would have been silly to have two Jane Goodalls.

Maybe next year, I'll consider dating someone from October 30 to November 1. Then we can do a quadruple costume.

I WAS SO HAPPY WHEN HALLOWEEN WAS OVER AND WE could concentrate on our project. Ian and I arrived at the perfect formula: he worked on the special effects for our presentation while I did the actual work. In the hallway on Wednesday morning, I finished the first paragraphs of our written report, about how texting was invented in 1992 when a computer programmer sent a message that said "Merry Christmas" to his coworker. Ian borrowed the class laptop and created a timeline (in green bubbles, as if all the key points were texts, which I had to admit was somewhat clever).

It was shocking we were able to concentrate AT ALL since JoJo and Rahul were communicating by drumming inside the classroom, and Cleo and Drew were "working" on the hallway floor across from us. They were trying to build some sort of Alexander Graham Bell transmitter, which looked ridiculously complicated. There was a plumbing pipe involved, and wood to nail together, and water. Cleo kept having to get more and more paper towels from the bathroom to wipe the floor.

She wasn't happy. When Cleo's not happy, she makes snorting noises like a baby dragon. And when you hear those snorting noises, you have to back off for a while. Because, you know: fire-breathing.

Drew didn't seem to get the warning signs. And if I weren't such a mature and empathetic person, I might have found the situation a teensy bit entertaining.

"Can you hold this?" he asked, sounding a little frustrated himself.

"Yes, Your Highness. As soon as I finish my Cinderella job here." Cleo snorted.

"Earth to Mya," Ian said, but I ignored him.

"Not that way," Drew said, once Cleo was helping again. Another snort.

"It's not going to work like that. You have to —"

"Mya?" Ian said.

"Wait," I hissed. "In three . . . two . . ."

"STOP TELLING ME WHAT TO DO!" Cleo threw the piece of plastic tubing into the middle of the hallway. "You're not the only one who knows how to do everything!"

She threw the water cup too, as she stomped off. Cleo had been throwing more things than usual since she'd started hanging out with Drew. He was definitely a bad influence.

"Whoa," Ian said. "How did you know that was going to happen?"

I rolled my eyes. "Because I have eyes? And a brain?" Guys were seriously thinking-impaired.

Drew was still standing in the middle of the hallway, staring in the direction Cleo had disappeared.

"So . . . do you want to look at the cartoon panels I did last night?" Ian asked tentatively, as if I might rip his work to pieces at any minute. Which I'd sort of wanted to do at the beginning of our session. But somehow, watching Cleo lose her marbles made me feel better about my own project partner.

"Yup!" I said brightly.

"I think they're perfect," I told him, once I'd had a look. Surprisingly, they were really well drawn, and he'd accomplished way more than I thought he would.

"Tomorrow, we can work on a script for the two of us," I said.

Ian seemed eager to follow instructions at that point, and everything was coming together exactly as I had planned. Hopefully Drew was watching and learning.

DAD SAID I SHOULD DO MY HOMEWORK WHILE I WAITED for Nanda at the skateboard park after school on Thursday, but it was impossible to think. There was horrible music blaring from a stereo that looked as if it had time-warped straight from the 1980s. Plus, I thought my sister was going to kill herself.

She zoomed right off the highest ramp. I could see that her skateboard was traveling faster than her body and she was just about to bail . . .

I shrieked, clapping my hands over my mouth.

Nanda didn't fall. She jumped off her board at the last minute and ran a couple of steps to catch up with it. Then she tucked it under her arm and sauntered over to me, all attitude. She may as well start designing her own tattoos, I thought.

"Did I freak you out?" she said, with the most annoying grin ever seen on planet Earth.

I glared at her.

"You should try it sometime. I could show you," she said.

Now she was being ridiculous. "I have homework."

"I think you're scared," she said.

"Scared you're going to get a brain injury."

"Awww. I didn't know you cared."

"I'll be the one stuck at home pouring pureed Toaster Strudels through your feeding tube."

She started making chicken sounds, but she had already thrown down her board. She rolled away too fast for me to catch her.

To: p.lwyn@hotmail.com
From: myamyapapaya1@gmail.com
Subject: Arteries in danger

Hi Mom!
Dad keeps saying "any day" for when you're going to come home. I'm so, so glad that Grandma's out of the hospital. That is amaZING! What's this paperwork you have to wait for, and why, why, why is it taking so long?

We need you around here because (a) no one can find the can opener and Dad keeps forgetting to buy one, so he's been using a camping knife to open soup cans, and sooner or later he's going to slice an artery. Also (b) Auntie Winnie's threatening to give me another cooking lesson. I guess if that happens we won't need soup anymore, so we won't have the sliced-artery problem, but you might have to pay for counseling sessions for me for years to come.

Plus, you should come home because we love you, obviously.

I read your email about the shrine, and about how you'd be happy to tell me more about the offerings once you're back. Don't worry. I won't do anything until then. Unless it's an absolute emergency.

Love, love, love,
Mya

I NEVER THOUGHT I'D BE THANKFUL FOR THE EXISTENCE of Nanda. But if I hadn't already endured eight years of her presence, I'd never have lived through babysitting the Sanders boys on Friday night.

Everything seemed fine when Mrs. Sanders left. "You can let them watch telly for a few more minutes, then choose a board game from the cupboard," she said. "After that, bath-y and bed-y." She had a high, little-girl voice, even when she wasn't rhyming.

The boys had matching white-blonde hair, like angels. The six-year-old, Damien, had soft curls that floated out from his head when he moved. And the older one, Danny, flashed a perfect little dimple when he smiled. Of course, I knew they weren't *exactly* angels, because I'd seen them fighting in the schoolyard. But I figured my natural way with children and my superior resourcefulness would solve any problems we might encounter.

H-E-double-hockey-sticks, no.

I'd heard their mother say one cartoon, then board game, bath and bed. They'd heard something different. Something more along the lines of: refuse to turn off the TV; kick Mya when she tries to take away the remote control; clap your hands over your ears and yell whenever she speaks to you; don't go anywhere near the bathtub; when she unplugs the TV from the wall, strip off all your clothes and race naked through the house.

I started with nice voice, then moved on to firm voice. But eventually I lost it. Just as I was yelling at them to get into the bath, or else . . . the doorbell rang.

I'm pretty sure that during my babysitting course, the instructor said not to answer the door at night. But (a) I didn't have my manual with me at that moment, (b) I wasn't thinking clearly and (c) any serial killer waiting outside would have been easier to control than the psychotic naked monkeys. So I opened the door.

Two smiling men in suits stood on the stoop, holding magazines about Jesus.

"Is everything okay?" the taller one asked. I'm sure they'd heard me screaming my head off.

"It's fine." I gritted my teeth as Danny made a howling, naked leap for the couch behind me. I could tell Damien was already plugging in the TV.

"Well, my name is Jonah and this is Andrew, and we're calling on you and your neighbors today with a fascinating article titled 'The World of Truth.' Would you or your parents be interested in reading this?"

He didn't wait for me to answer. He kept right on talking. Behind me, Damien and Danny were fighting over the remote and Damien was crying, and I had this horrible feeling that Mrs. Sanders was going to come home from her class to find me in the middle of a religious conversion while her kids pounded each other in the living room. She'd probably call the police and have me checked into a mental hospital.

"I have to go," I told the suit-men, a little desperately.

The tall one kept talking.

"Maybe you can come back tomorrow and talk to Mrs. Sanders."

I didn't want to be rude, but he was still blathering, and Damien was now screaming like Danny might be amputating body parts. I started to slowly close the door.

"Please, take this. We can stop by again —"

I managed to shut the door on them after accepting their magazine, with its picture of a flowing-haired prophet on the cover. Holding it, I stomped back to the couch and stood over the two wrestling boys.

"Who was that?" Danny said, with his forearm pressed against Damien's chest. Damien was crying so hard he couldn't talk through his snot.

Inspiration struck. I held up the magazine.

"It was Jesus," I said. "He wants you to be nice to your brother, and to have your bath."

Maybe Jesus was actually hanging around just then, because IT WORKED! Both boys scrambled up, wide-eyed, and ran for the tub. They were already naked. They stood silently beside me while I ran the water and tested it for perfect babysitter standards. They got in together, they used soap and they HUNG THEIR TOWELS ON THE RACK AFTER-WARD. By the time Mrs. Sanders got home, they were in bed.

My mind was . . . kaboom. Blown.

I had witnessed a miracle.

"We had the most empowering fellowship," Mrs. Sanders said, in her little-girl voice. It turned out the Sanders were serious Baptists and she had been at her weekly women's Bible study. I had already buried the magazine in the recycling, and now I couldn't decide whether she might think that was good (I was pretty sure the men at the door weren't Baptists) or sacrilegious (because Jesus was on the cover). Jesus is Jesus, I was also pretty sure. But not quite sure enough to mention the magazine.

Anyway, Mrs. Sanders kicked off her low black heels and reached into her purse for her wallet.

"How much do I owe you?"

"Twenty dollars?" I had been planning to ask for eight dollars an hour, not ten, but I deserved danger pay.

"Ooooh," she cooed. "I only have a ten. Would that work?"

What I wanted to do: scream, cry, throw myself at her shins and wail, "Why me?"

What I did do: nod and smile. Then I got the heck out of that house before the miracles wore off. Those boys were NOT worth the money. And at this rate, I would never, ever, ever be buying a phone.

CLEO CALLED ME ON SUNDAY AFTERNOON TO PLAN our next Kids for Social Justice meeting. As in, she actually called me. On my landline. That hadn't happened for so long, I almost fell over when Nanda said the phone was for me.

The first thing Cleo told me was that she'd had bad dreams ever since she'd seen *Razor*.

"That's terrible. Poor you," I said, because United Nations diplomats need advanced social skills and "I told you so" is never helpful in building relationships.

Then Cleo said, "I have news about Drew!"

For the briefest moment, I thought she might have regained her senses and realized Drew has the maturity level of a labradoodle. Unfortunately . . .

"He wants to join KSJ as a permanent member!"

No breakup scene in sight.

"Great." Saying that word felt like putting a fork in my eye, but these were the things one did for friendship. At least, these were the things *I* did.

"Do you have ideas for our meeting next week?" she asked.

"Do you?"

"I've had NO time," Cleo said.

"Well, I thought we could each write to a government of a place like India, Vietnam or Brazil. All those countries use child labor."

"Perfect!"

"I had my own child labor experience this weekend," I

said, all set to launch into my nightmare babysitting story.

"Oh, I've got to go. My cell's ringing!" Cleo said. "But we'll catch up at school tomorrow!"

It was probably Drew calling her cell. Or JoJo.

I wondered how many people were on the official list of "calls that would make Cleo hang up on Mya." The number seemed to be growing.

WE SWITCHED FROM TOASTER STRUDELS TO TOASTER waffles—a major advancement.

Unfortunately, Dad left for work ridiculously early on Monday morning, and then Nanda caught me placing pieces of my waffle into a bowl on Mom's shrine.

"What are you doing?"

"Making an offering," I said.

"Mom told you not to touch her shrine."

"She did not."

"Did too."

She didn't *exactly*. She said she wanted to talk to me about it first, that's all.

"How do you know?" Nanda had been reading my emails, that's how she knew. I could see it on her face.

"Because that's what she would say!"

"She was glad I asked about the shrine," I countered.

Mom and Dad always said that Nanda and I could explore Buddhism or Christianity, or any other religion, if we were ever interested.

"Yeah, but you're supposed to talk about it again when she gets home. Not start messing with her stuff."

"I'm not messing with her stuff! I'm praying!" This sounded less convincing because I was yelling, which was Nanda's fault for being so seriously annoying, which was yet another good reason to learn Buddhist prayers and meditation. I was going to need them to get through the next six years of my dysfunctional home life.

Nanda folded her arms across her chest. "So are you a Buddhist now?"

"None of your business." I pushed past her and stomped upstairs to get ready for school. But the truth was, I had no idea. Mom always said Buddhism was more of a philosophy than a religion. So did it matter if I prayed to Buddha and to God at the same time?

Nanda switched back to yelling, this time from the bottom of the stairs. "I'm telling Mom!"

"Fine! Go right ahead! It was only a toaster waffle!"

They were surprisingly good, those waffles. It was a real sacrifice to save part of mine for Buddha. Hopefully he appreciated it.

I GUESS GOD AND BUDDHA WERE BOTH BUSY WITH THE cell-phone issue and weren't available to help me out at my KSJ meeting. Things didn't go so well.

I'd found a video of Kailash Satyarthi, the Nobel Prize winner who freed thousands of kids from slavery in India.

I arranged for Ms. Martinson to let us use her projector for our meeting, and I created a list of charities working on the issue, so if we planned a bake sale or something, we could donate the money.

That was A LOT OF WORK. Which I had done, apparently, for the sake of ungrateful people with the attention span of baboons. Ian and Drew whispered all the way through the video. Even though Cleo was sitting right beside Drew, she didn't shush them once, and I don't think it would have been too much child labor on her part to tell them to shut up.

Halfway through, Ian said, "Could we maybe skip the rest of the video and talk about—"

"No!" I hissed. "This is important."

Drew elbowed him. "There's no free speech at Social Justice meetings," he said.

"That is NOT true," I said.

"Seems like it," Drew said.

Everyone stopped watching the screen. They all turned their heads back and forth between us, as if they were watching a tennis match.

On the screen, Kailash Satyarthi was talking about moving from anger to ideas to action, but all I had was anger and no ideas. I jabbed at the power button and the screen went black.

"Maybe we could plan another bake sale?" Cleo said, so quietly that you practically had to use one of Alexander Graham Bell's inventions to hear her.

"I vote we have a giant doughnut sale," Drew said.

"Dunk tank," someone else said.

"Hot dog eating contest."

When I looked at Cleo for help, she was STARING AT HER PHONE!

"Wait, I've got it!" Drew shouted. "Bikini car wash!"

I grabbed my stuff and left the room. Sometimes, even at the UN, diplomats had to excuse themselves. That's what the poor countries did in 2015 after Australia and other rich countries refused to discuss paying to clean up after climate change events like hurricanes and typhoons. The representatives from the poor countries stood up and walked right out of there. Sometimes you had to stick with your principles, even when you were surrounded by baboons, and not get sidetracked by Australia or bikini car washes—or traitor friends either.

I was halfway down the hallway when Ian called my name. "Mya, I didn't mean . . . the video was boring, but I still think . . ."

I ignored him and headed for the library, where none of the baboons would ever find me because they were probably illiterate. They wouldn't even be able to make car wash signs without me.

"I hope they catch pneumonia," I muttered as I plunked myself down in a study carrel.

Then I quickly took it back, in case Jesus or Buddha were listening.

IAN CALLED ON MONDAY NIGHT TO APOLOGIZE FOR leading the meeting astray. He actually called twice. The first time I refused to talk to him, but the second time I remembered about (a) my future with the UN and (b) forgiveness. So I talked to Ian, he apologized, and next thing I knew, he'd arranged to come over after dinner on Tuesday to work on our communications project.

Most. Embarrassing. Evening. Ever.

First, Dad kept acting like a freak. When the doorbell rang, he followed me into the hallway.

"Hi," Ian said when I opened the door.

"Hi," I said.

"Hello there, young man," Dad said, in a weirdly deep voice. "Ian, is it? Nice to finally meet you." And then he shook Ian's hand.

ARGH! Couldn't he follow our social lead? Couldn't he tell that "hi" was the only appropriate greeting at that moment, and that it should preferably have been given from much farther away, without physical contact?

I almost turned into an amoeba and slid through the crack under the door.

It got worse.

Dad offered juice and Ian said YES, even though I was raising my eyebrows at him like crazy to get him away from Dad. But Dad poured him a glass of mango juice, and it turned out that Ian had never tasted a mango before. (How was this even possible?) He thought the juice was delicious. Then Dad launched into Myanmar stories, because of course mangoes grew on trees in Myanmar, and there were all sorts of other tropical fruits sold by children balancing baskets on their heads. The kids were cute, but he failed to mention a few problems.

"Hello? Child labor? Illiteracy?" I said. You'd think, as a lawyer, he would notice these things.

"The funniest thing, though," he said, ignoring me as he poured Ian a second glass of juice, "is that when we were there a few years ago, all those little street kids had cell phones!"

I must have had my jaw hanging open at that point, because he stopped and looked at me with his eyebrows wrinkled. "What?"

"STREET KIDS IN MYANMAR HAVE CELL PHONES AND YOUR OWN DAUGHTER HAS NO ABILITY TO COMMUNICATE WITH HER FRIENDS?" I was so appalled I could barely get the words out.

Dad chuckled and shook his head. "As soon as you have a job in sales, I'll get you a phone," he said.

My own father thinks I should leave school to wander the streets with bananas on my head. As if that would make me more deserving of a phone than going to university, joining the United Nations and saving the world from war.

The universe was a cruel and unfair place.

I finally dragged Ian away from his new best friend and got him into my room, where we were supposed to work on our project. I had tidied BOTH halves of the bedroom in the afternoon, knowing a guest was coming. But apparently Nanda had been in there while we were discussing mangoes and child labor and telecommunications.

She had left Pennybear (dirty, disgusting, one-eyed

Pennybear) AND a pair of her underwear (disgusting, already-worn underwear) on MY bed.

Her underwear was pink.

With purple ruffles.

I almost had an aneurysm.

Fortunately, I was a step ahead of Ian, so I was able to scoot forward and plop myself onto the bed, hiding the world's most offensive panties under my butt. It was the first time I had ever wished for a bigger butt, the better to hide dirty underwear beneath. In fact, at that moment, I was wishing I had a butt so massive that I could have covered up the undies and Pennybear at the same time.

Possibly I wasn't quite as smooth as I thought, because Ian looked at me funny. He took a couple steps into the room and then turned in a slow circle, like he didn't know where to put himself.

"Just sit down," I said. "Let's get this done."

When I said "just sit down," I meant in a normal place. On the carpet. On the edge of Nanda's bed. On the desk chair, even. Those would have been reasonable choices. But no, Ian sat right beside me. RIGHT beside me. And I couldn't move, because of the underwear hidden under my butt. So there I was, Pennybear on one side, giving me his sly stare (honestly, I wanted to smack that bear), and Ian on my other side.

Ian folded himself to sit cross-legged on the bed, and his knee touched mine.

I was suddenly frozen in place.

He turned toward me and I could tell by the half-smiling, half-nervous, entirely goofy look on his face that he knew his knee was touching mine. It was there ON PURPOSE.

In my head, warning lights flashed. It was as if I were in the nuclear war room and someone had started the count-down and total world annihilation was going to happen on the count of ten unless I, top UN negotiator, stopped the clock, but I couldn't think properly. Five . . . four . . .

Ian leaned in. He had a tiny smear of mango on his upper lip.

. . . three . . . two . . .

"There's a bathroom just down the hall," I blurted. "In case you need to go. Or to wash your hands. Or something."

Ian turned bright red. He scrambled off the bed, tripping over his own crossed legs, and practically ran down the hall.

I took a deep breath. I didn't need to ponder that situation any further. I would draw no conclusions about what could have happened or almost happened. I would simply accept the facts as I saw them, the way an objective UN leader would do. There didn't need to be any wild speculations.

As soon as Ian was out of sight, I fished the underwear from under my butt and put them in the hamper, then stuffed Pennybear under Nanda's pillow, punching him once or twice for good measure. I was sitting on the carpet in a much more normal position by the time Ian returned. I had our notebooks open and our pencils sharpened and even part of our final script written.

Ian had been in the bathroom for a long time, actually. Maybe it was the mango juice.

THOUGH THE WHOLE SITUATION HAD LASTED ONLY A nanosecond, I couldn't stop thinking about the way Ian had leaned toward me with that goofy look on his face. Every time I pictured us together in my room, my insides turned bubbly. And not in a good way. Or if it *was* the good way, the way people talked about in books, I wanted nothing to do with it.

It wasn't only my stomach. As I tried to sleep, my brain spun through alternate scenarios.

For example, if I'd known Nanda would try to ruin my life by strewing her panties and Pennybear around our room, I could have checked on the state of things while Ian was busy bonding over mango juice. If I'd only done that, the entire bed/knee/lean situation would never have happened.

OR I could have stopped in the doorway of our bedroom and yelled at Nanda to come and clean up her stuff. Even if Ian had seen the underwear, he would have known they weren't mine.

OR I could have stayed silent when Ian leaned toward me. Then I would have known for sure what he intended, and I wouldn't be possibly the only seventh-grade girl in the world who'd ruined her first kiss opportunity by hiding underwear under her butt and talking about bathrooms.

The last option made my insides feel bubblier than ever,

so I stayed awake even longer, wondering if the bacteria on Pennybear's fur had given me a gastrointestinal disorder.

When I finally got to school on Wednesday morning, half-asleep and still confused, I saw Cleo and JoJo standing together outside homeroom. Cleo and JoJo, with their boobs and their leopard-print iPhone cases and their sparkly lips. Seeing them sitting together, all glittery, I felt as if they might have all the answers.

"You guys have to help me," I said.

They both sat straight up, grinning.

"Ian came over yesterday to do homework," I said.

"Homework," Cleo repeated, drawing quotation marks in the air. "That's not what I heard."

"What did you hear?!" I couldn't imagine Ian talking to Cleo about kissing me, but he might have talked to Drew. And then Drew would have told Cleo. And now Cleo and JoJo were both giggling . . .

"Nothing happened!" I blurted.

The giggling stopped. Cleo, eyes wide, leaned toward me slightly and lowered her voice. "But did he try?" she said.

I was going to tell them what really happened. But suddenly I felt small and lip-gloss-less in front of them. How could I confess that (a) I had nose alignment questions, (b) I'd panicked and sent Ian running to the bathroom or (c) I hadn't wanted to kiss him in the first place?

"Did he try to kiss you?" Cleo asked again.

"He did."

They both squealed.

"But it was SO awkward. I couldn't take it!"

They giggled again, and I wasn't sure if they were laughing with me or at me.

"He had mango juice smeared on his lip," I blurted.

JoJo laughed so hard she snorted, but Cleo froze, staring at something over my shoulder.

I turned around, and of course it was Ian standing there, and of course he'd heard everything. He looked as red and steaming as a pot of Auntie Winnie's chicken curry.

He stomped past us toward the classroom, avoiding eye contact.

All three of us stared after him.

"This is why you're supposed to text things," Cleo whispered. "It's more private."

"I DON'T HAVE A PHONE!"

Ian turned back to glare at me. Then our homeroom teacher appeared in the doorway. "Everything all right out here? Are you girls planning to join us today?"

Intentional blindness and sarcasm. More things they learned in teacher school.

And of course—because I was the unluckiest person in the universe and because God was apparently punishing me for things I'd done in a past life—when we got to English class, Ms. Martinson announced that we were going to spend it working with our partners on our projects.

"Mustard and catch-up time," she called it. Which was a teacher joke, and therefore not actually funny.

Ian and I retreated to the hallway. Sometimes we would

push two desks together out there, but this time we sat on the floor with a big, gaping chasm between us. He handed his papers across to me without speaking. He'd done some more cartoons over the weekend and he'd added a lot to our script.

"Wow. This looks great," I said, scanning the pages. There were obvious problems, but as a future professional diplomat, I knew it wasn't the right time to explore them.

When I glanced up, Ian folded his arms and glared at me. I could feel my face flushing. Which made me angry.

"Look, I wasn't the only one talking to people."

Glare.

"I didn't even bring up the issue of . . . the issue. Cleo *asked* me. She obviously knew something, so you obviously told someone you were going to do something!"

Mr. Kapoor stuck his head into the hallway from the math room, looked at us pointedly and closed his classroom door. Ian was still glowering at me.

"This isn't all my fault!" I hissed.

"I wasn't going to kiss you," he whisper-yelled back.

"Oh, really?"

"Really."

"Fine."

Then it occurred to me that maybe he was telling the truth, he'd never planned to kiss me, and I'd misinterpreted everything. I considered curling into a ball and rocking back and forth until the end of the day.

"I'll finish this project with you, but we are NOT friends," he said.

"Fine."

Ian wasn't finished. "You run that club, and you look after your sister. I thought you were different."

"I *am* different!" To my horror, my eyes welled up. This was something that absolutely, completely could NOT happen during my UN career.

My traitor throat closed too, and I couldn't explain how different I was. I didn't even own a cell phone and I wasn't allowed to wear lip gloss! How much more different could I get?

"I would never try to kiss someone who talks behind other people's backs," he said.

Which made it seem as if he HAD intended to kiss me. But even though he was CLEARLY waiting for me to say something, I had all these quivery and mad and embarrassed thoughts swirling around and they practically made my head explode.

"Never," he said.

I had to turn the other way, take deep breaths and look only at my paper for a while.

When I finally looked up, he was drawing more cartoons.

"Do you want to borrow a pencil sharpener?" I asked.

"No."

If he'd said yes, we might have patched things up, but he didn't, AND he was wrong about me, AND the whole situation was not definitely, entirely my fault. So I fixed his stupid presentation script, better than he could have fixed it, and he drew things, and I counted the number of days until our horrible project was over for good.

Seven.

ANY NORMAL PERSON WOULD HAVE GONE TO BED AND pulled the covers over her head after all the craziness with Ian. Especially since I had a stomachache after dinner on Thursday. But as an above-average, responsible and resourceful human being, I wasn't about to let a boy ruin my life.

I sat down at the computer in the living room and began researching issues for future KSJ meetings. (Cleo was no help at all anymore, so the survival of this club was up to me.)

Dad and Nanda walked through the room behind me, on their way to soccer practice.

"Are you on the computer again?" Dad asked. "Why don't you invite a friend over one of these days?"

"If I had a cell phone, I could be *texting* my friends like a normal person. Since I *don't*, I'm looking for new KSJ topics."

He snorted. "Look up cobalt mining in the Congo."

Before I could type it in, he put a hand on my shoulder. "Did you get any emails from Mom today?"

"Not today."

I was going to ask why he wanted to know, but he was already heading out the door, and also my search results appeared.

Whoa. My brain almost exploded, and NOT in a good way.

Apparently, tons of people in the Congo had died in mining accidents. Plus, there were civil wars happening, people were starving and kids were getting trained as soldiers. It was all because of a mineral called cobalt. Which would henceforth be known as "cobalt, the mineral that ruined Mya's life."

And Thursday, November 9th, became the day Mya's state of happy ignorance ended forever.

I suddenly understood why people say ignorance is bliss.

But because I was someone who cared about the future of the world and about other people, *and* I was the president of KSJ and therefore needed to have high moral standards, I added the issue to my paper: cobalt in cell phones.

According to the Internet, cobalt was a mineral used to make electronic components. All the big companies needed it, and they sometimes bought it from unstable places like the Congo, where cobalt mining used child labor and caused wars.

Seriously, I felt the living room rock beneath me.

This was the worst news ever.

This was the end of all my dreams.

Also, just as I reached the depths of despair, I stood up from the computer desk and felt something . . . wet. I looked behind me, and there was a tiny damp spot on the chair.

My stomachache began to make sense.

I went straight to the bathroom to confirm, and yes. It looked as though Nanda would have to wear her real shin pads to all future soccer games. Mom's box of back-ups would be needed for other things.

It took a lot of trips from the bathroom to my bedroom to get organized. First, I had to get clean underwear. Then back to the bathroom to change. Then back to the bedroom. Then back to the bathroom one more time to make sure I'd buried my stained underwear beneath so many layers of tissue and toilet-paper rolls they would never be found.

It was all too much. The fight with Ian, the discovery of cobalt, the arrival of—this was the only time I was ever going to use this word, ever—menstruation. I went straight to bed and put my pillow over my head. When Nanda got home and asked if I was sick, I pretended to be asleep.

Dear Family,

Try not to worry about me. I'm moving to the Arctic, where I will live simply and peacefully. Alone in my igloo, I will no longer need to worry about how every single one of my friends has a cell phone and is texting behind my back ALL the time and knows everything at least twelve hours before I do and is probably laughing about me right now. I won't care anymore, because I will be tranquilly melting snow over my whale-oil lamp. *Synthetic* whale-oil lamp. I may need to arrange delivery by bush plane every month or so. Maybe the pilot will be a woman and she can bring other supplies too, because I'm planning to stay there for a few years, and there probably won't be a drugstore nearby.

AAAAAAAARRRRRRRGH!
This whole period thing is even ruining my escape fantasies.

Dear Family,

Scratch that. There is too much white in the Arctic. I am moving to the Amazon. Where jaguars will probably smell blood and hunt me down before my first month is over. It was nice knowing you.

This seems like a pointless death.
Eaten by jaguars. Swallowed by the Amazon.
No one will ever know what happened to me.
I'd rather die for a cause, I think.
Or maybe not actually die.

Dear Family,

New plan. I am retreating to the top of Lynn Peak. Did you know a real-life hermit used to live there? Like him, I will be existing without technology. And since there's probably not a lot of food up there except huckleberries, which are too sour, I will be launching a hunger strike. I will not be coming down the mountain until (a) political prisoners everywhere are freed, (b) I have my own ethically produced cell phone and (c) all of my friends have graduated and moved to other cities, so no one remembers my current humiliations. Please give Mom and Grandma my love when they return.

Tragically yours,

Mya Panone

Mya

I WENT TO SCHOOL EARLY ON FRIDAY MORNING, EVEN though I still had a stomachache. I cornered Cleo as soon as I found her. "Can we talk about KSJ?"

She groaned, not even bothering to look up from her screen.

"What are you playing?"

"Unicorn races."

Sure enough, there was a miniature pink unicorn on her screen, dodging past trees and leaping over fallen logs. As I watched, a turquoise unicorn caught up, nipping at her heels. Then, as she reached an open field, the turquoise one passed her.

"Noooooooooooo," Cleo cried.

As her unicorn trotted past the finish line in second place, she said, "That's the third time in a row she's won."

"Who?"

"JoJo!" As if it should have been obvious that JoJo was a turquoise unicorn.

"Where *is* JoJo?"

"She stayed home. She has a headache."

I wasn't sure video games were the best headache cure, but I wasn't a complete social idiot, so I said nothing. Plus, I had to focus on the screen as Cleo showed me how to customize unicorns.

"So," Cleo said eventually, "what did you want to talk about?"

"KSJ. I have a meeting idea, but I don't know if you'll like it."

Her phone buzzed. "Drew's in the gym. He wants to show me his jump shot before class," she said. "Whatever subject you choose will be fine!" She called the last part over her shoulder, already hurrying down the hall. Because jump shots were oh-so-interesting and much more important than child slavery.

She was going to feel terrible when I told her about cobalt.

MYA'S MOST SUCCESSFUL STIR-FRY EVER

(Chopping assistance provided by Auntie Winnie, who did not need to make SUCH a big deal about skipping her Scrabble group for my sake, but who was otherwise quite helpful.)

    1 package vermicelli rice noodles
    1 tablespoon oil
    4 teaspoons crushed garlic
    3 tablespoons grated ginger
    1 pound ground chicken
    ¼ cup fish sauce
    ¼ cup honey
    ½ teaspoon ground anise
    1 pear or Asian pear, diced
    4 green onions, diced
    4 tablespoons cilantro, chopped
    ¼ cup chopped peanuts (optional)

Soak noodles in boiling water for 3 minutes, then drain. Heat oil in a large frying pan on medium-high. Sauté garlic for about one minute, until golden. Add ginger and chicken and fry until chicken is cooked through. Add fish sauce, honey and anise, and fry for 1 or 2 minutes without burning (or caramelizing either). Turn off heat and stir in remaining ingredients. Serve over noodles.

Next, accept praise and adoration from your family.

SINCE IAN WASN'T TALKING TO ME, I DIDN'T KNOW HOW much of our presentation script he'd finished. I decided to do a whole new one myself, which is what I'd expected to do as soon as Ms. Martinson announced we were partners. But Ian had been more useful than I thought, and now the double work seemed somehow worse.

On Saturday evening I spread everything on the dining room table and started to organize. Here's how our project was going to work: we had a three-page written report about the development of texting, a copy of our script, and Ian's comics to hand in as our written portion. For our class presentation, we would read our script aloud. In between, Ian would show some comics. On the screen behind us, while other things were going on, our slide show would summarize the main points. A lot of our slide show was done in Ian's bubble sentences, like texts. I hadn't edited them yet, but they were pretty good.

> Some people think texting changes the way your brain works.

> Texting is quick and difficult to track. So people have used it to organize demonstrations and even overthrow governments. #Egypt #ArabSpring #LookItUp

> Because it's so cheap, texting has allowed poor people in Africa to access online courses.

> Texting can divide our attention. That's a problem if you're driving. Or even walking.

That's where some of Ian's cartoons would come in.

While I was putting the finishing touches on our conclusion, I heard Dad in the kitchen, talking on the phone. He was using his secret-telling voice. So of course I stood up from the table and slid closer to the doorway.

"Not since Wednesday," he murmured.

Pause.

"Yes, that's when it hit."

Pause.

"Who knows how long it will take them to get things up and running again? This is Myanmar we're talking about!" His voice rose briefly, then dropped again.

"If you could try the relatives . . ."

"Of course. I'll let you know right away."

Under normal circumstances, I would have pretended not to be listening. But this was too important. I accosted him as soon as he hung up.

"MOM'S GONE MISSING!?" If he hadn't heard from her since Wednesday, she'd been gone for three days. Weren't you supposed to get Amber Alerts out in the first hour?

"She's not missing," he said quickly.

"But you haven't heard from her."

"There was a storm, which knocked out the phone lines."

"What kind of storm?"

"A typhoon. It —"

"A TYPHOON!" My mother had been struck by a typhoon, and he was hiding the news from me?

"What's a typhoon?" Nanda appeared in the doorway, looking from me to Dad and back again.

"A storm," Dad said.

"A big storm," I added.

"A hurricane?" she asked.

"No, this was a small typhoon. Like the way a thunderstorm is here," Dad said.

"Can we order pizza for dinner? And eat with flashlights and pretend the power's out?" Nanda asked.

"That's —" A ridiculous response to the disappearance of your mother, was what I was about to say, before Dad rudely interrupted me.

"A wonderful idea," he said. Then he gave me a pointed look, and I zipped it. Though I still glared at him. If certain people had a missing mother, those people had the right to know.

The front door banged as Nanda went back to the driveway, her primary hangout since the skateboard appeared in her life.

"I don't want to worry her for no reason. Your mom's not missing. It's just that the lines are down. We'll hear from her anytime now," Dad said.

"We'd better," I told him, and I would have said more if our phone hadn't started ringing again right at that moment.

If it had been Mom, it would have been SO perfect. But I could tell from Dad's voice that it wasn't.

"Tomorrow?" he said. "Of course. I'll let her know. She really enjoyed spending time with your boys."

And suddenly I knew who was on the phone. It was Mrs. Sanders!

I leapt in front of Dad, waving my arms, slicing my throat with my finger, basically standing on my head trying to signal him NOT to agree that I would babysit. But he'd suddenly gone blind.

"There's nothing on the calendar. I'm sure that will be fine."

"Daaad!" I protested, as soon as he'd hung up.

"You said it went great last time. I thought you were saving up."

What was I supposed to tell him? That I'd lied, and the Sanders boys were miniature psychopaths? Plus, he'd already committed me. In Dad's world, once you'd committed to something, you did it.

"I thought you might need my help with Nanda," I tried weakly.

"We'll manage," he said.

"With Mom missing, you might have to spend extra time. You know, calling the Red Cross. Making posters."

"Mom's not missing. You're being overly dramatic."

"Because I could babysit Nanda while you handle the situation."

"Are you finished? I'd like to get the pizza ordered."

And that was that.

Doom, with extra pepperoni.

To: p.lwyn@hotmail.com
From: myamyapapaya1@gmail.com
Subject: Missing in action

Hi Mom,

Dad says you're not missing, it only SEEMS like you're missing because you have no electricity or Internet connection. But that's practically the same thing! This is the twenty-first century, and if you don't have a phone or a GPS device or Internet, it's as if you've been erased from the face of the Earth!

Please, please, please make them restore power quickly and then get on the first plane out of there.

Maybe you can adopt some Rohingya refugees on your way out of the country? I could move to the downstairs bedroom and Nanda could stay with Auntie Winnie. For months, if necessary. Then a whole Rohingya family could share the upstairs bedroom.

(Dad says this is both illegal and unreasonable, and he's already donated money to aid agencies, but personally I think direct action would be equally effective.)

Missing you tons,
Mya

THOSE SANDERS BOYS WERE THE MOST CONNIVING, devious creatures ever born, and I was never, ever baby-sitting again. And then Ian . . . aaaaargh!

There I was on Sunday afternoon, the world's most chipper babysitter standing at the stoop. *Ding-dong.* I was greeted by a slightly flustered Mrs. Sanders, who flitted out the door before I could ask where she was going and when she'd be back. But that was okay. I was determined to do a better job this time.

"What should we play first?" I plastered on my biggest smile. I was going to remain patient, use a firm voice when necessary, and refrain from threatening innocent children with eternal damnation.

The boys looked at each other, then smiled up at me, their matching, freckled faces enough to melt any heart.

"Hide-and-seek," they said.

It was perfect. I counted to ten, the boys hid, I found them after a suitable amount of "searching" and then we traded roles.

For the second round, they insisted on blindfolding me while I counted. No problem. I even counted super-slowly, to give them extra time to hide. I still found them within seconds. They were terrible at hiding, I thought. Maybe their mom never had time to play this game with them.

Then it was round three. This time, I was to be blindfolded and tied to the chair. I balked. "How am I supposed to look for you if I'm tied to the chair?"

"We'll just tie you loosely," promised Damien.

"You'll escape like Houdini, and then you'll find us," said Danny.

"We've been reading about Houdini." Damien smiled up at me.

I was still hesitant, so they took their turns first. Danny tied Damien lightly to the chair and blindfolded him, then we hid while Damien escaped. Danny went next, and he escaped his ties and rounded us up in mere minutes.

How could I refuse to take my turn when they'd both done it? Especially when (a) they were behaving much better today, and (b) I wanted to be the fun kind of babysitter. The one they'd beg their mom to call. The one who earned extra tip money at the end of each shift.

So I sat down. They blindfolded me. They tied me to the chair.

I could feel that they were tying the knots too tight, but there was one of them on either side of me by that time, and those little monsters were stronger than they looked. And probably Boy Scouts too. Before I could say "Houdini died a horrible death," I was permanently tied to the chair. They may as well have lifted me onto a spit and spun me above a raging fire.

And of course THEY'D PLANNED THE WHOLE THING! The entire game of hide-and-seek had been a plot to get me tied to that chair. As soon as I was incapacitated, they scampered off to the kitchen. Once I wiggled my blindfold off, I saw they'd climbed on the counter to reach the top shelf, and were making potions with sugar and hot chocolate powder and chocolate chips. It was disaster in slow motion. I could practically see a chocolate-covered tsunami looming over the house. I yelled at them to stop, but I couldn't DO anything because I was TIED TO A CHAIR.

I pulled at the ropes until my wrists burned, I yelled at them again, and I even tried breaking the chair—because it seemed better to have Mrs. Sanders come home to find ruined furniture than an incapacitated babysitter and her house turned into a chocolate war zone. But none of it worked, and I ended up a sweaty, red-faced mess.

That's when the doorbell rang.

Damien raced from the kitchen, chocolate powder in his hair and liquid chocolate smeared on his face. His hands looked as if he'd been sculpting mud.

"Do NOT answer," I said.

I admit, I was torn about this, because I was certainly in need of rescue. But letting six- and eight-year-olds answer doorbells while you were incapacitated was *not* recommended during my babysitting course.

Obviously, Damien ignored me and whipped open the front door.

And the WORST possible person was standing there . . . Ian.

With his little brother. Apparently, Ian's little brother Aiden was friends with Danny Sanders. Aiden wanted to play video games, so Ian walked him over.

I had the worst luck in the entire universe. I must have been a truly terrible person in a past life in order to deserve this.

"What are you doing?" Ian asked. At least he didn't immediately ask why I was tied to a chair, but STILL.

"Babysitting," I said.

"Playing hide-and-seek!" Damien said.

"We're done that game now." I smiled. It was more like gritting my teeth, but I tried really hard to make it look like a smile. "So you can untie me."

"Hmmmm . . . maybe later," Danny said. Then he grabbed Ian's brother. "Come see our potions!"

Ian untied me. While laughing.

"How did —"

"I do NOT want to talk about it."

He dropped his voice to a whisper. "Why are you baby-sitting these two? They're insane. Their mom keeps asking me to babysit, but I keep making excuses."

I rubbed my wrists and glared at him. "It's your fault."

"How can it be my fault?"

"It's your stupid 'multi-pronged strategy' idea."

He looked completely confused.

"Look, I need to convince my dad to get me a cell phone. That means proving that I'm responsible and reliable, and that I can help pay for it. I babysat once, and it was horrible, but then my dad volunteered me again."

"But why do you have to babysit?" he asked. "Why don't you look after Nanda?"

"Because my dad says that's my responsibility as a sis-ter and he won't pay me, even though I only asked for five dollars an hour!"

That's when the Sanders boys dropped a glass bowl on the kitchen floor. Ian refrained from mentioning that the boys were a billion times more impossible than Nanda and entirely not worth the money, AND he said nothing about the disastrous kiss situation. For those reasons, I allowed him to stay and help me clean up the zone of destruction that was the kitchen.

He dragged his brother out of the house minutes before Mrs. Sanders arrived home.

"How did everything go?" she asked brightly, looking around the living room. Except for the skipping ropes still sitting beside the chair, things looked reasonably tidy.

"Great!" Damien and Danny said from behind me, probably wearing their demonic angel smiles.

I managed to smile and nod while I waited for Mrs. Sanders to pull another measly ten dollars from her wallet.

"Maybe next week?" she asked.

But I was already on my way out the door, and I would never, ever, EVER go back to that house. Ever.

Outsmarted by two deviants, and then "rescued" by Ian.

Whenever I even thought about it, my head exploded. Kaboom!

PART V

NINE WEEKS WITHOUT MOM

O N MONDAY MORNING, IAN BROUGHT ME A PACKAGE of multicolored sticky notes.

"I thought these might be useful for organizing our presentation," he said.

Sticky notes aren't what I would have chosen as a peace offering, but I accepted gracefully. "Thanks. And thanks for . . . you know . . . the whole chair untying thing."

"Anytime," he said.

"Well, it won't be necessary anytime, because I will never again be babysitting those monsters."

Ian laughed. He had a surprisingly nice laugh.

I took a deep breath. "I also wanted to apologize for that whole scene with JoJo and Cleo. I didn't mean to . . ." Then I sputtered to a stop because my throat was closing up, and I could feel my face burning at approximately six billion degrees. Ian had also turned scarlet, which made me feel a little better.

"Whatever," he said.

In a fit of generosity, I reminded him of the lunchtime KSJ meeting.

My stomach started bubbling again when he said he'd come, but that's just because I'd done a LOT of preparation for our meeting and I wanted it to go perfectly.

THE MEETING STARTED OUT PRETTY WELL. WE HAD A good turnout. Ian sat in the front row. Cleo was there (though she'd brought Drew, who sort of cancelled her out). There were a dozen other members, and most of them seemed to be listening.

I had photos of child laborers, which I passed around to the group. I had the addresses of phone-company CEOs. I'd even asked Ms. Martinson for a flip chart so we could brainstorm protest ideas after we'd finished writing our letters.

"All these companies need cobalt for the rechargeable batteries in cell phones and laptops," I explained to everyone. "Half the world's cobalt comes from the Congo, where there are forty thousand kids working in mines."

"Says who?" Drew asked.

"UNICEF. The kids spend all day underground, and they get paid hardly anything."

There was a murmur as everyone absorbed this.

"We'll write our letters first, then we'll brainstorm more protest ideas. If some of you feel you have to make the moral choice to give up your cell phones, you can write about that in your letters."

Drew snorted. "People aren't going to give up their phones."

"Some people might," Ian said.

"If they want to live in the dark ages, like you," Drew said, leaning forward to punch his shoulder. Apparently Ian is another member of the Eternally Phoneless Society. Which is good for the state of the world, and especially the Congo.

"Everyone has to be quiet now, so we can write," I told them, before the meeting turned into a wrestling match.

Drew snorted. "Write exactly what you say to write?"

I glared first at him, then at Cleo. If she was going to bring him, she should at least try to control him.

She shrugged. "He has a point. We should hear both sides."

Which was like an oil company suggesting we listen to anti–climate change "facts." Of course she wanted to hear both sides. She wanted to keep her pink unicorn!

"Fine." I looked at Drew.

"Giving up our phones seems extreme," he said.

"And African kids working in mines? That doesn't seem extreme?"

"Mya," Cleo said, as though I was the one causing problems.

"It can't hurt to write letters," Ian said. Which was nice of him.

"Agreed," Drew said, pretending he was Mr. Mature. "But I think we should put our own opinions into our letters, and not threaten to give up our phones if we're never going to do it."

The whole group was murmuring. A couple of people nodded and one girl actually slid her notebook into her backpack. In another minute, they were all going to leave and Congolese children would be slaving away in cobalt mines forever.

I gritted my teeth.

"Of course."

"Of course what?" Drew asked.

"Of course our letters should express our own opinions. Obviously."

I took a deep breath and thought about all the global treaties the UN had negotiated. They'd convinced countries to do things like stop making nuclear weapons and save Earth's ozone layer. Getting tons of world leaders to sign major agreements probably wasn't easy.

"I'm handing out fact sheets," I told everyone. "You can refer to these as you write. If you want." Seriously, the whole situation was horrifying, and reading these facts would definitely, for sure, convince them to give up their phones, and then things could get back to normal AND we could save the Congo.

THIS was the type of thing I'd be known for in my UN career.

Except it didn't work.

It took forever for people to write their letters, and we only had about five minutes at the end of the meeting to brainstorm. Then all of their ideas were seriously small-scale.

"Raise money for UNICEF," one of them said.

"Write to governments so they can create an organization that will keep track of where cobalt comes from, and whether there's child labor happening." Which was way too long to even fit on the flip chart.

"BOYCOTT CELL PHONES," I wrote, finally, in big red

letters across the bottom of the page. But by that time the bell was ringing and lunchtime was over.

I sort of hoped Ian would want to talk privately about the fact that we were the only seventh graders without phones, but Drew put him in a headlock and dragged him from the room. Arrgh.

Then—double-arrgh—I saw Cleo checking her texts as she got ready to leave.

"JoJo's feeling better," she told me as she passed.

Once everyone had gone, I tore the brainstorming sheet off the flip chart and crumpled it up. I didn't even put it in the recycling bin. I was so frustrated, I stuffed it right in the garbage.

BY THE TIME DAD GOT HOME FROM WORK ON MONDAY night, I'd already fed Nanda leftover noodles and put her to bed. Dad and I sat on the couch together for a while watching CNN, the most depressing channel in the history of the universe.

"Rough day?" Dad asked during a commercial.

I couldn't look at him because I'd gotten something in my eye during CNN's update on the Rohingya refugee camps in Bangladesh, where people did not exactly have sparkling futures—or proper food or health care either. Cobalt. Child labor. Imprisoned writers. Refugees. It didn't seem like our KSJ meetings could solve ANYTHING.

I took a deep breath. "It's impossible to fix all these problems."

Dad nudged my shoulder. "Even for a future UN diplomat?"

"Especially for a future UN diplomat."

"What's going on? This doesn't sound like my world-changing daughter," he said.

"But I'm NOT changing the world. That's the whole point. Nothing's changing!" It occurred to me that my dad, as an environmental lawyer, should understand this. "How do you go to work every day and try to protect the environment when global warming keeps happening, and animals are dying like crazy, and your whole existence is practically useless?"

My voice squeaked at the end of all that, which may have been why Dad got a strange look on his face.

"Small steps," he said finally.

"What?"

He muted the TV. "Sometimes, you have to concentrate on the things you can accomplish," he said. "We can't fix everything. But if people take small steps in the right direction, the world will slowly shift. That's what I tell myself, anyway."

Then he seemed a bit embarrassed and he turned the sound back on.

"Small steps," I repeated.

He shrugged.

I didn't want small steps. I wanted huge, impressive leaps that brought global adoration. Still, it wasn't his most terrible advice ever. Our KSJ donations were at least feeding a few people, and those few were probably happy to have lentils and rice, especially if the organizers running the refugee camps were better cooks than my dad, and no one had to eat caramelized broccoli.

Small steps.

I resolved to think more deeply about this. But not at that moment, because the people on TV were arguing about politics. It was so painful to watch that I actually went to bed without being reminded.

To: p.lwyn@hotmail.com
From: myamyapapaya1@gmail.com
Subject: Disappearing from the face of the Earth

Hi Mom!
I don't know if you'll get this or not. As soon as you manage to phone, I need to tell you about KSJ. The whole club's gone crazy, and not even your poop-sandwich technique is going to make it right again. Plus, Cleo's practically abandoned me. She's shirking her responsibilities, and she shouldn't get off the hook just because Ian offered to help with the next meeting. Ian's a surprisingly reasonable person. Not that he matters. It's just that we're working on a project together. If it weren't for that, I wouldn't care.

I hope you and Grandma are okay. If you get this, give yourself huge kisses for me.

Love,
Mya

WHEN I WAS REALLY LITTLE, GRANDPA WOULD TELL ME about his year alone in Canada. He came by himself, before Grandma, Mom and Auntie Winnie, so he could get a job and rent an apartment. His first month, he was hired at a meat-packing place, and he wore five layers of clothes because it was freezing and he didn't know about long underwear.

All week, Grandpa would save up his change. Then he'd drive to Seattle on the weekend to call home from a pay-phone. At the time, there were no phone lines connecting Myanmar to Vancouver.

How crazy is that?

I was feeling a bit like Grandpa. Mom and Grandma seemed a long, long way away.

Around our house, things were NOT getting better. My entire multi-pronged strategy had failed. In fact, my entire life had disintegrated.

a) Mom was incommunicado.

b) My best friend loved unicorns, Drew and JoJo better than me.

c) I'd practically sold my soul to earn twenty bucks from Mrs. Sanders, which might buy me enough root beer to drown my sorrows but definitely wouldn't buy me a cell phone. Which anyway I maybe didn't want anymore because: cobalt.

d) Refugees.

e) I WAS OUT OF SUPPLIES. The important kind, also known as shin pads.

I NEEDED A MULTI-PRONGED STRATEGY TO DEAL WITH the fallout from my multi-pronged strategy. And I couldn't even start with the most important issues, such as the absence of my mom and the existence of child slavery. According to the Internet ("Information for Tweens: Understanding Your Body," which was the most disturbing site EVER), periods could last from two to seven days. I was on day four or day five, depending on whether Thursday counted. I had one pad left. What if it wasn't enough?? I'd already searched all of Mom's drawers and purses and found nothing.

Other problems might have been more important to the global village, but this one seemed more immediate.

I followed Cleo outside after school, thinking about my lack of supplies and considering—possibly—asking her to help with the situation. But as she hatched baby dragons on her way out the door, I imagined how our conversation would go.

MYA: Can you come to the store with me after school?

CLEO (not looking up from phone): Why?

(Mya whispers in her friend's ear. Cleo looks appalled.)

CLEO: OMG. That's so embarrassing!

MYA: I know, right? So can you come?

CLEO: I can't! We're in the middle of a twelve-hour super-spawn. If Drew and JoJo hatch more eggs than I do, I have to dress entirely in pink tomorrow. Can you imagine?

(Mya grabs her friend's phone and crushes it into cobalt dust under her heel.)

I didn't ask her. Besides, Drew and Ian arrived on the front steps and invited us to hang out for a while. Cleo said yes, but I had to pick up Nanda, who—as always—was responsible for ruining my life. Not that I necessarily wanted to hang out with them anyway.

I WASN'T ALLOWED TO WALK TO THE STORES ON Broadway by myself, and I definitely couldn't ask Dad to buy me anything. Look what happened when he saw wrappers on the bathroom floor. He'd practically discussed it with the whole world. If I sent him to the drugstore, he'd post it on Facebook or announce it in court.

Also, every time I even thought about asking, I went purple and my mouth turned into the Sahara Desert.

There was really only one option.

I called Auntie Winnie when I got home from school.

"Just heading out the door," she said. "I haven't heard anything from your mom yet, but I got a message through to one of the aunties. She's going to check in at the guesthouse."

"Great," I said. It *was* great. But not helpful.

There was a long pause, during which I heard Auntie Winnie's keys jingling.

"Anything else you need?" she prompted.

"Can you . . . take me to the store tonight?"

"Oh, honey, I'm meeting friends tonight. Are you out of ingredients?"

"Sort of."

"Just throw some lentils and an onion in the slow cooker, and pour in a couple jugs of chicken stock. You'll have lentil soup in time for a late dinner."

"I just —"

"I've got to go. Tell your dad I'll call as soon as I hear."

And that was the end of the world's least helpful conversation. I did put the lentils in the slow cooker, though.

Then, after I got Nanda an after-school snack, I put my shoes on.

"Finish your strudel and then watch TV for a while, okay? I have to run an errand."

"What kind of errand?"

"I have to pick up something for dinner."

"Is it beep-sparagus?"

"No!"

"Good. Can I come?"

"No!" That was all I needed. My sister following me around the drugstore, asking questions. "And don't go outside, either. Watch cartoons or something, and I'll be home super fast." I didn't give her any more time to object. I was already closing the front door behind me as I said those last words.

The drugstore was only a couple of blocks past the school. I fast-walked the whole way. But then I saw Ian's mom in the vitamin aisle, and obviously I couldn't buy anything while she was there. Luckily she didn't spot me. I read greeting cards until I was sure she'd left. Then I scoped the aisles for anyone else I knew (clear) and went to choose my product.

Aaaaaah! There was an entire wall of feminine hygiene products. Green boxes and pink boxes, yellow boxes and purple boxes. Blue plastic bags full of smaller blue plastic squares. Pretty much everything except red boxes, not that I had time to notice. I grabbed a package randomly and hightailed it down the aisle.

But what if they were the wrong ones?

I ran back and grabbed two more packages for good measure. Then I walked straight to the till, looking neither left nor right.

There was an old lady ahead of me in line, buying fiber supplements. Not that I would ever look at what embarrassing things other people buy, because that would be a serious invasion of privacy. But she fished change from her purse SO SLOWLY I thought the end of the world might happen before she came up with six dollars and forty cents.

Finally, it was my turn. There was no one behind me. I dumped my three boxes on the counter.

The clerk picked up each one with her thumb and forefingers, ran it across the scanner and put it into a plastic bag. A translucent plastic bag. I should have brought my own reusable one.

"Can you double-bag it?"

As she obligingly wrapped my products in two layers of Earth-killing plastic, I blurted, "Those aren't for me."

Because that was the kind of mature, together, cusp-of-adulthood person I could be. The kind who could embarrass herself and pollute the Earth, all at the same time.

I handed her my twenty-dollar bill. "Keep the change," I said. Then I bolted.

There was another drugstore a few blocks down. Which is where I would be shopping for the rest of my life.

I HAD TOLD NANDA VERY CLEARLY TO STAY INSIDE while I was gone. If that imaginary judge and jury appeared beside me, they would rule unanimously in my favor. But on the way back from the drugstore, as soon as I turned the corner to my house, I saw my sister riding her board up and down the sidewalk. She wasn't even wearing her helmet.

"Nanda!" I yelled at her. Then I pointed to the house.

She saw me. Your honor, let the video replay prove that she turned her head, saw me and chose to continue riding.

As I was inhaling, ready to start hollering at her again, she went for one more trick at the end of our driveway.

She missed it.

Missed it disastrously.

Her board flew out from under her, her feet flipped up and she flew across the sidewalk. From half a block away, it seemed to happen in slow motion. My vision narrowed until all I could see was the arc of her body. All I could hear was the smack of her skull on the concrete.

"Nanda!"

I sprinted the rest of the way and dropped to my knees beside her.

"Nanda?"

Her eyes were closed. I leaned close to check that she was breathing. She was, but she didn't respond when I called her name again.

There was no one else on our street. The houses were closed and quiet as if we'd warped into *A Wrinkle in Time* and IT was turning everything wrong.

"I need help!" I yelled, but no one appeared.

It felt horrible to leave Nanda lying there.

"I'll be right back," I promised. Then I raced inside and grabbed the phone.

When I returned, phone in hand, she hadn't moved.

"What is the nature of your emergency?" a voice asked.

"Ambulance!"

I was connected to a woman who asked a billion questions. Was Nanda conscious? (Maybe? Her eyelids had fluttered. Or I'd imagined it.) Was she bleeding? (No.) Was she in a safe place? (Yes.) Could she answer questions?

I finally lost it. "I don't know! I can't tell because I'm stuck on the phone with you! Are you sending an ambulance or what?"

"An ambulance is already on its way," she said. "Now —"

But I hung up on her so I could grab Nanda's hand and tell her everything was going to be okay. (Was it?)

I grabbed the phone again and dialed Dad's work number. His assistant, Tracy, answered. He was in court, she said, and couldn't be disturbed.

"Could you tell him to call me? It's an emergency."

Then I hung up on her too. Who else could I call? Auntie Winnie was out for dinner and I couldn't remember her cell number. I dialed Cleo's house and her cell, but there was no answer at either. "Nanda's hit her head," I told her voice mail. "I called 9-1-1."

Just as I hung up, the phone rang in my hand.

"Cleo?"

"Mya?" It was Mom's voice.

"Mom! Are you okay? We heard about the storm."

"I'm okay. Grandma and I are coming home —"

"That's great, Mom! I can't hear you, there's a siren. Nanda hit her head —"

I dropped the phone on the grass as the ambulance screeched to a stop and two paramedics leapt out. For a few minutes, it seemed as if Nanda and I were on the set of a TV movie that we weren't old enough to watch.

"Mya?" Her forehead was strapped to a rolling bed by this time, but Nanda's voice sounded normal.

She was going to be okay. My lungs filled with air and I wondered how long I'd been holding my breath.

"Can you get the cat? There was a cat —" she said.

I looked up at the paramedics. "We don't have a cat."

"Sounds like she gave her head a good bang," the woman said.

"Probably a mild concussion," the man said. "Where are your parents?"

"Mom's in Myanmar and Dad's in court." Equally unhelpful.

"Hop in with us," the woman said. "They'll check your sister at the hospital, and a social worker can help you contact your family."

"You can call them from the waiting room," the man added.

"I don't have a phone!" I wailed.

At that moment, I didn't care about unicorns or dragon eggs or child slavery. All I wanted in the world was to call Dad, and for him to come and make things better. Once we were inside the ambulance and it had lurched into motion, I said a prayer that Nanda would be okay. Then I said another to Buddha, just in case.

When I opened my eyes, Nanda was still muttering about cats. From across the stretcher, the woman paramedic gave me a sad, sympathetic look, as if I were an orphan. When she passed me a tissue, I realized my cheeks were wet.

Then I realized something else. I was no longer holding the plastic bag. My three boxes of supplies were sitting somewhere on the sidewalk.

I burst into full-scale tears.

"She's going to be okay," the woman said.

Hopefully that was true. But I'd started the day with a list of problems, and not a single one was solved. Everything kept getting worse.

By the time we reached the hospital, Nanda was making sense again. At least, she was making as much sense as she did on a daily basis, which wasn't a lot.

"I wish you'd gotten there a few minutes earlier, Mya. I did that trick perfectly when no one was watching."

"If I'd gotten there a few minutes earlier, I would have killed you. You weren't supposed to leave the house."

"That would have been beep-beep-sination."

It took me a minute to figure out she was saying *assassination* in the way only my sister, out of seven billion people on Earth, would say it.

I could have killed her right there and then, but (a) she'd come a little too close to dying without my intervention, (b) nurses are probably trained to prevent family beep-beep-sinations in the waiting room and (c) I kind of loved her beeps.

Nanda was stuck at the edge of the hallway while she waited for an examining room and a doctor. The paramedics had said I could sit on the end of her rolling bed. They'd gone to get coffee from the vending machine, with promises that a social worker/nurse/doctor/random-person-in-uniform would arrive soon.

"Wait until I tell the social worker that Dad can't be reached and we've been eating Toaster Strudels and frozen waffles for weeks now," I said to Nanda.

"Why?"

"Probably we'll be sent straight to foster care. I *told* Dad I needed a cell phone and more than thirty minutes of screen time a day."

Nanda looked horrified.

"I'm kidding. They're not sending us anywhere."

"Promise?" she asked. Suddenly she seemed small, lying on her big white rolling bed, and I would probably have promised her anything. Those Sanders boys with their dimples and blonde locks had nothing on my sister.

"I promise. And Dad will be here soon."

In a shocking turn of events, she wiggled down the bed so she could grab my hand.

Dad always said that Nanda looked up to me, but this was practically the only time in history it seemed to be true. It was sort of a nice feeling.

I squeezed her fingers in mine. "Your skateboarding *is* impressive, even if it goes wrong occasionally."

"Dad will never let me skateboard again."

"He will. He'll probably ground *me* for life, though."

"Why?"

"For going out and leaving you there."

For a minute, I sat and stewed in my own shame.

From our perch at the edge of the hall, we could watch the action in the waiting room. And it was mostly horrible. A baby screamed its head off while its mother said "shhh, shhh, shhh," and bounced up and down like a demented robot. Another mom held a bowl as if her son was going to throw up at any moment. Near them, a small boy sat with a bandage pressed against his arm. I could see blood seeping through.

Our current situation *was* my fault, even though there were extenuating circumstances. "I was supposed to be taking care of you."

Nanda reached up to pat my shoulder. "You're taking care of me now," she said.

My cheeks were annoyingly wet again, but I smiled at her.

It was a nice bonding moment. But would it be shallow to say that I was beginning to regret the fact that I was sitting on all-white sheets? Even though not much had happened lately, bodily-function-wise, the website *had* said four to seven days.

Just as I started to worry, the sliding glass doors to the waiting room slid open. Cleo and her mom walked in.

Thank you, powers that be.

Cleo's mom wore her slightly scary, serious police-officer look. But when she spotted us at the entrance to the hallway, her expression melted.

It was amaZING to see someone we actually knew.

"Poor things!" She hurried over to give me a hug, then she practically smothered Nanda in mom-love. Nanda burst into tears and I couldn't even blame her, because I felt like I might do the same thing. It was such a relief to have a responsible adult in the room.

I said hello to Cleo, who was hanging in the background.

"Your dad's on the way," she said, holding up her phone. "Mom got ahold of him."

"Thanks."

"Want to get a hot chocolate?"

I didn't answer, because (a) there was the white sheet issue and (b) I wasn't sure I was on speaking terms with Cleo. I still wanted to grab her phone and crush it.

And I sort of wanted to kick her in the shins too. This was a new feeling for me. I wasn't usually given to fits of violence.

But Cleo didn't wait for my answer. She bummed money from her mom. And since Nanda seemed well taken care of, I stood up (no stains) and trailed Cleo across the waiting room to the vending machines. Then I spotted the restroom sign right beside them.

"Come with me." I tugged Cleo into the bathroom and made her guard the stall door while I had the longest pee ever. When I came out, as I was washing my hands, I saw the dispenser.

SANITARY NAPKINS, it said. Which was another of the Worst. Names. Ever. Seriously, it was right up there with *menstruation.*

"Can I borrow money?" I asked Cleo.

She followed my gaze to the machine.

"Seriously? Why didn't you tell me?" She passed me the coins.

"Maybe because I didn't want Drew and JoJo and the whole world knowing?"

"That's a little harsh," she said.

Something was jammed in the machine. I put the coins in, but the dial didn't turn properly. Eventually, I bashed it with the side of my hand. Which was not effective, and also painful.

"Are you, like, mentally okay?" Cleo asked.

"THIS IS ENTIRELY YOUR FAULT!"

"What are you talking about?" she hissed. "How is this my fault?"

"If you'd come to the drugstore, the way I was going to ask you to, and the way any reasonable best friend would, you could have watched Nanda on the sidewalk outside while I went inside, and she wouldn't have been skateboarding without her helmet and she wouldn't have brain damage!"

It actually hadn't occurred to me to have Cleo watch Nanda on the sidewalk, but it would have been a good plan. I'm sure I would have thought of it at some point.

"You didn't even ask me!" Cleo protested.

"Because you were too busy breeding unicorns!"

"Dragons!"

"Exactly!"

At that point, the bouncing mom with her wailing baby pushed open the door. She looked back and forth between us, then left.

"All you care about is your stupid phone and stupid Drew. We don't even hang out anymore."

My last words got muddled by snot, NOT something that happened to UN negotiators. I forced myself to calm down and take a deep breath. Which almost made me miss Cleo's next words.

"Well, we can hang out as much as you want now, because Drew and I broke up."

"You broke up?" It didn't make me quite as happy as it would have if her phone had fallen in the toilet. But close.

"He farts. In my presence."

I forced myself to hold my angry face. "You can't dump your friend when you have a boyfriend and then expect to get her back when the farting gets too much for you."

"If she's your best friend, she'll love you no matter what," Cleo countered.

"Well, maybe JoJo's your new best friend."

"Don't be ridiculous," she said, which made me ridiculously happy.

At that moment, Cleo's mom walked in. "Everything okay here?" she asked. Bouncing lady had probably messaged her with mom-telepathy powers.

Cleo and I nodded silently.

"Mya, the doctor's with Nanda now," she said.

I beelined for the door. But I turned back and stood in front of SANITARY NAPKINS again. Then I looked pointedly between Cleo and the machine. I handed her the money. If she wanted to prove we were really best friends, I knew exactly how she could start.

I was halfway across the waiting room when Dad burst through the doors, his face red and his hair sticking up like crazy.

"Mya!" In what seemed like two giant steps, he was at my side, folding me into a squishy, slightly sweaty hug. "Where's Nanda? Is she okay?"

"Mm fdff wrf nnda," I said from against his lapel.

"What?" He backed up a step but kept hold of my shoulders, as if I might disappear otherwise.

"The doctor's with Nanda. Cleo and her mom are in the bathroom."

Still with a hand on my shoulder, he stepped to the desk and asked to see Nanda. It seemed to take forever, and I swear I could see more of his hair stand on end with every passing second, but eventually we were ushered down a hall and into a small examining room. There, a young, pony-tailed doctor perched on a chair with a clipboard in her lap. Nanda sat across from her on an examining table, smiling, sucking on a lollipop, and looking ready to skateboard again at any moment.

She submitted to a giant Dad hug, but in her mind, the crisis was obviously over . . . UNTIL the doctor said that for three days, there would be no TV, no loud music and no video games. Also, absolutely no skateboarding or soccer for at least a week.

"But I'm better!" Nanda wailed.

The doctor smiled and patted her knee. "We have to give that head some time to heal. Just to be safe."

Define safe. That's what I wanted to say. Keeping Nanda locked inside for a week was going to be mortally dangerous for the rest of us.

Once the doctor left, Cleo's mom peeked in. "I left Cleo in the waiting room. If everything's going okay, we'll head out," she said.

Dad gushed all over her. "I can't thank you enough," he said.

"I didn't do a thing," she said. "Mya had it all under control. She knew exactly who to call, and she stayed right next to her sister the whole time."

"Good job, kiddo," Dad said.

I admit, it was an emotional moment. I *might* have cried, if I hadn't cleverly spotted a golden opportunity. (Sensing these moments is an important skill for UN negotiators.)

"It would have been a *lot* easier with a cell phone," I said.

Dad rolled his eyes and turned to gather Nanda's things. Still, he didn't say, "No. Never. Not until you're thirty-eight." I interpreted that as progress.

While Dad's back was turned, Cleo's mom beckoned me closer. She quietly passed me a plastic bag. "Hospital gift shop," she whispered.

Even though she hadn't said a single one of the forbidden words (because Cleo's mom is more evolutionarily advanced than ordinary parents), I'm sure I turned bright red before I even peeked inside.

"Thank you."

"Things will get easier when your mom gets back," she added, more loudly.

"Oh, Mom called!" In all the chaos, I'd completely forgotten. "She called as the ambulance arrived at our house."

Dad whipped around. "Is she okay?"

"She's coming home! She and Grandma are coming home."

I couldn't be sure exactly, but Dad's eyes might have gotten a little runny at that point.

Cleo's mom and I tactfully looked away.

Mom called again a little while later. This time, she was in Hong Kong, where she and Grandma were staying the night so Grandma could rest. Dad gave her a full update.

She'd been panicking since she talked to me. I guess I dropped the phone while an ambulance screamed in the background, which might have implied we were all dying, but I can't be expected to do *everything* perfectly.

ON FRIDAY, AUNTIE WINNIE PICKED UP MOM AND Grandma at the airport while Dad and I played Snakes and Ladders with Nanda because my sister has no inner resources and can't entertain herself quietly for a single second. I pretended she was a foreign ruler who had narrowly escaped a coup and had to live in hiding until she could reclaim her throne (which would only be done through my heroic interventions). It made Snakes and Ladders more entertaining, even though it was a serious stretch to imagine Nanda as a foreign queen. Especially when she had popcorn in her teeth. Plus, she cried when she hit the snake on the ninety-eighth square.

Mom and Grandma and Auntie Winnie arrived in an avalanche of suitcases and scarves, moments before I staged my own coup.

It was possible there was more than one person in tears after that, but as there was no photographic evidence, this could never be proven.

Eventually, everyone sat down in the living room. Dad handed out cups of tea and I dished Mom and Grandma bowls of lentil soup, because even though it seemed about a decade ago, it had only been two days since I'd put lentils in the slow cooker. (Dad had been pretty impressed when we arrived home and dinner was ready. I could tell Mom and Grandma were impressed too, when Auntie Winnie bragged about my new cooking abilities.)

I told Auntie Winnie I liked her scarf, even though I didn't, because that's how warm and fuzzy I was feeling about the world.

When they'd finished their tea and soup and boring chit-chat, Mom suggested that Grandma might want to lie down.

"How long are you staying?" I asked.

"That brings me to a big announcement," Mom said. "Grandma's going to move in with us. She'll use the downstairs bedroom."

My bedroom. That's what Mom meant. The downstairs bedroom I was *supposed* to have, if my family had acted like a normal twenty-first-century family instead of insisting that we all sleep on the same floor of the house.

I felt as if Mom had just thrown *me* off a skateboard.

Then I happened to glance at Grandma, and she looked ... embarrassed. I couldn't tell if she was embarrassed because she needed us to take care of her, or embarrassed because she was basically stealing my rightful bedroom. But still ...

"That's great. It will be nice to have you here, Grandma." I got the words out, even though they tasted like imitation-chocolate strudel.

Nanda was cheering, of course, because Grandma always handed out a constant stream of candy like a clown in a parade.

Mom beamed at both of us. Which sort of helped with the taste in my mouth.

Anyway, it turned out that Grandma wasn't ready to be tucked into bed. She wanted to give presents. So the massive suitcases were flipped open, and out came a burst of sandalwood, a much less appealing waft of dried fish and some serious souvenirs.

Gifts for Mya	Gifts for Nanda
• Parasol (pink)	• Parasol (orange)
• Sandalwood powder (sort of like makeup, if you're from Myanmar)	• Elephant marionette
	• Spinning wooden top
• Jasmine perfume (!!!)	• Tamarind candies
• Tamarind candies	• T-shirt with an elephant on it

Even though there were not exactly the same number of presents for each of us, mine were obviously better, so I hardly noticed the discrepancy. I even managed not to argue when Mom said I could only wear the perfume on special occasions and not to school. (As a negotiator, one has to choose the best moments for addressing sensitive subjects.)

The presents took a long time, especially since Nanda insisted on trying her marionette. She immediately tangled the strings, and Dad practically had a stroke while sorting them out again. Eventually, though, the puppet was saved and my sister sent to put on her pajamas.

Dad moved to sit beside Mom with his arm around her shoulders while he made seriously embarrassing googly eyes at her.

Grandma was probably disgusted. She started to pull herself off the couch.

"I have one more present," Dad said.

Grandma sat back down.

"You didn't go anywhere," I said. "Why are you giving presents?"

"Well, this one's special. It's something your Auntie Winnie helped me arrange this week."

Auntie Winnie looked strange. If I didn't know her better, I'd have said she was nervous.

"You've handled a lot while your mom was away," she told me.

Dad nodded. "You really took responsibility around here, and you looked after your sister. You acted like an impressive young woman."

The word *woman* made my cheeks go hot, even though THAT wasn't what he was talking about.

Right about then, I began to hope, even though I was scared to hope in case my present was a new pair of peace-sign earrings, which would have been a CRUSHING disappointment.

Dad reached down beside the couch and pulled out . . .

I stopped breathing.

I honestly thought I might be hallucinating. Or that Dad might say "psych!" and pass the box to Grandma.

But he didn't. He passed the CELL-PHONE BOX to Auntie Winnie, who passed it to me.

TO ME!!!!!!!!!!!!!!!!!!!

Cue balloons, unicorns, dragons and trumpets.

Thank you, God, and Buddha.

"We'll have to discuss some guidelines," Mom said.

I barely heard her. I hugged Dad so hard I probably broke his ribs, and kissed Auntie Winnie so many times that my lips would taste of makeup for weeks. I didn't care. I wasn't going to say or think anything bad about Auntie Winnie for the rest of my life because she was one of my favorite people in the whole world. Then I kissed Mom and Grandma, because I was basically overflowing with love. People who said you couldn't buy happiness were wrong. THEY WERE WRONG! Happiness came in a box.

Guess who?

Who?

I GOT A PHONE! MY OWN PHONE!

Mya?

YES!!!!!!!!!!!!

OMG, I'm so happy to hear from you. Drew and I got back together after I saw you at the hospital, but we just broke up again.

ACK! I need all the details.
I'm going to call you right now.
On my NEW PHONE!!!!!!!! 😊☹️

CLEO AND JOJO WERE SO EXCITED TO SEE MY PHONE ON Monday morning. Especially since Mom took me to the mall on Sunday and we got a gold glitter case! (Leopard print was completely yesterday.)

While we were squealing, Drew and Ian arrived at homeroom.

"Mya got a phone!" JoJo told them.

"What about the cobalt?" Drew asked, with the world's most annoying smirk on his face.

JoJo stared at him as if he were an alien, but I felt a little quiver in my stomach. He was right. One weekend with technology and I'd completely forgotten about child slavery and unsafe working conditions.

"I'll write a letter," I said weakly.

He snorted.

"If phone companies are big enough and smart enough to change the way the whole world communicates, they can figure out better ways to get cobalt," Cleo said, because she was an awesome best friend.

Drew still looked superior. And I had to admit, it was the teensiest bit possible that he was right in our KSJ meeting and boycotting cell phones was an unreasonable idea.

But even though I was a future UN diplomat, and therefore should have chosen the high road, I couldn't bring myself to apologize. He was just too annoying.

"Small steps," I blurted.

"What?"

"If we get everyone to take small steps, like writing their phone companies about cobalt, then the world will slowly change."

"Actually, I read that some phone companies are going to work directly with miners. Maybe we can have fair trade cobalt, like we have fair trade chocolate and coffee," Ian said.

"You researched cobalt?" Drew asked incredulously.

Ian flushed. "I thought we might talk about it more, at future KSJ meetings."

I almost hugged him. Instead, I clapped my hands together (gently, because I was still holding my phone in its gold glitter case). "I'll write a letter to encourage fair trade cobalt. I'll write tons. Masses of letters."

"Me too," Cleo said.

Even JoJo nodded.

So it was settled. Although I thought I might send emails instead. Because I could send emails FROM MY NEW PHONE!!!

TEXT REVOLUTION
Mya Parsons and Ian Winters

IAN:

Text messages weren't invented until the 1990s, but now they're huge!

MYA:

Well, they're actually tiny. Small messages on small screens. But there are a lot of them!

People around the world will send 23 billion texts today. That's 8.3 trillion texts a year.

IAN:

Two-thirds of North American teens text every single day. More than they use phones, more than they email and even more than they hang out with their friends face-to-face.

In North America, kids 12 to 17 send and receive an average of 30 texts each day.

IAN:

It turns out that teen brains especially love "rewards"—like the little beep that happens when a text comes in.

MYA:

Sorry, I've got a text. Go on without me . . .

IAN:

If our brains are trained to respond to that beep, texts can seem more urgent than they really are.

MYA:

Pardon? I was busy. Give me one more second . . .

Texting drivers are 23 times more likely to crash.

MYA:

I'm just kidding. Of course I'm paying attention!

IAN:

Mya's demonstrating how texting can distract us if we're not careful.

MYA:

But texting affects us in other ways too. To use a random example, let's say your friend gets a new cell and starts texting instead of calling or meeting in person. Your relationship might change because of the way she's communicating.

IAN:

People also worry that if you only read texts, you might think only surface thoughts, instead of deep ideas. And researchers have shown texting makes people quicker, but sloppier.

Wha? U kidding me? My brain is on 🔥. No way I make mistaken.

IAN:

That's all the bad news. There's good texting news too!

MYA:

A British study found that kids who text have better reading skills. And in Israel, researchers showed that texting can help teens deal with anxiety and depression. Texting makes it easier to open up about your feelings.

IAN:

Texting can also change the world.

Big protest downtown. Meet at the square, asap!

IAN:

Texting is quick, cheap and hard for authorities to track. People have used texts to organize

demonstrations, and even help overthrow
governments.

Seriously. #ArabSpring

MYA:
Compared to phone calls and email—not to
mention smoke signals—texting is new. So
new, no one really knows what it can do. We
think it might eventually . . .

IAN AND MYA:
Change the world!

OUR PRESENTATION WAS AMAZING! IT WENT PERFECTLY! We were so excited afterward that Ian and I grabbed hands in the hallway and jumped up and down. Also, there was a brief moment *after* we stopped jumping but *before* Ms. Martinson called us back inside when Ian KEPT HOLD-ING MY HAND.

This may have been purely coincidental, so I didn't leap to conclusions.

I also vowed not to discuss this with anyone because I was NOT the type of person who talked behind other people's backs.

I would simply note the event for posterity.

And also for my biography, which people would be begging to write after my fabulous and world-changing UN career, during which I would solve all refugee problems and outlaw slavery and child labor, and free imprisoned writers too, in my spare time.

Acknowledgments

My husband, Min, was born in Yangon, Myanmar, which is 11,995 kilometers, or 7,453 miles, or an enormously gigantic distance from where I grew up in the small town of Creston, British Columbia. The fact that my fourteen-year-old daughter and twelve-year-old son actually exist is therefore miraculous. But they do exist, and they handle their Asian-Canadian identities (and their communications technology) with less angst and more grace than Mya.

While this book is not based on either of their experiences, they were kind enough to allow me to borrow a few real-life events (ahem . . . the metal water bottle). They were also kind enough to read the manuscript and comment on life at the juxtaposition of two cultures.

Many, many people helped me create *Mya's Strategy to Save the World*. A huge thank you to my family, both the Creston side and the Yangon side, for reading, suggesting and giggling. Thank you to my late mother-in-law, Joyce Kyi, for teaching me to cook the food of Myanmar. (And apologies for the simplifications I've made to her recipes.) Thank you to my husband, Min, for giving me the time and space to write, and only occasionally practicing happy birthday on the accordion while I'm trying to concentrate.

Thank you to my fabulous writing group, the Inkslingers: Rachelle Delaney, Kallie George, Christy Goerzen, Stacey Matson, Maryn Quarless and Lori Sherritt-Fleming. My agent, Amy Tompkins, has rooted for Mya since the first sample chapters, and the team at Penguin Random House—Lynne Missen, Margot Blankier, Shana Hayes, Peter Phillips, Five Seventeen and Sarah Howden—has been absolutely dreamy.

I wholeheartedly, thankfully acknowledge the Canadian Council for the Arts and the BC Arts Council for making the writing of this book possible.

And thank YOU for reading! Especially if you've read all the way through these acknowledgments, which is something only true book people ever do. In the words of Mya, you are amaZING!

Author's Note

The issues researched and discussed by Mya and her KSJ club are real.

The government of Myanmar recognizes 135 ethnic groups within the country, but the Rohingya aren't one of them. They're considered illegal immigrants, even though many have lived in Myanmar for generations. In 2017, facing persecution by the military, hundreds of thousands of Rohingya fled across Myanmar's border to makeshift refugee camps in Bangladesh.

It's hard to know how to respond to such a major crisis. Our family has donated through UNHCR, the United Nations Refugee Agency. Doctors Without Borders and Save the Children are also actively supporting the Rohingya.

Mya's concerns about cobalt are valid as well. The mineral is used in lithium-ion batteries, which are in turn used in smartphones and laptops. Activists accuse major technology companies of buying cobalt without investigating claims of child labor. If you'd like to know more, check out Amnesty International's website and the organization's campaign to have cobalt supply chains monitored more closely. Consider writing a letter to your favorite (or least favorite) technology company.

It's all about those small steps . . .

TANYA LLOYD KYI is the author of more than twenty books for children and young adults. She's married to the world's only occupational therapist from Myanmar (or so he claims), and they live in Vancouver with their two children (one of whom owns a cell phone with a glittery case). She's been known to eat both Ohn No Kauk Swe and toaster strudels . . . sometimes as part of the same meal.

www.tanyalloydkyi.com
@tanyakyi